Praise for Melissa Schroeder's
The Accidental Countess

"wow! Wow!! WOW!!! I love it!"

~ *Karen Kelley, Close Encounters of the Sexy Kind, Brava*

"I loved this book, and had a great time reading it."

~ *LeeAnn, Coffee Time Romance*

"If THE ACCIDENTAL COUNTESS is the beginning of a new series, then color me ecstatic to be in on the ground floor.. Melissa Schroeder has now been added to my list of favorites, and I'm heartily glad to recommend her newest, THE ACCIDENTAL COUNTESS. *Man, can that girl write!"*

~ *Amy Cunningham, Romance Reviews Today*

"Schroeder has crafted a touching and tender story with characters you can't help but love. This book has everything--heartfelt emotion, passion, and intrigue that will keep you eagerly turning the pages till the hankie-worthy ending."

~ *Kristina Cook, To Love a Scoundrel , Zebra*

"Hats off to Melissa Schroeder for one of the most amazing books that I've ever read. It was full of enough suspense, romance and humor to set the book writing industry on its ears... I gladly give this book a 5 angel and Recommended Read review."

~ *Missy, Fallen Angel Reviews*

"The emotional connection between Sebastian and Colleen is so richly woven that the readers find themselves enthralled waiting for them to have the happy ending they so deserve. Melissa Schroeder is always on my "must be read list" and The Accidental Countess is a perfect example why!"

~ *Melissa, Joyfully Reviewed*

The Accidental Countess

Melissa Schroeder

A Samhain Publishing, Ltd. publication.

Samhain Publishing, Ltd.
512 Forest Lake Drive
Warner Robins, GA 31093
www.samhainpublishing.com

The Accidental Countess
Copyright © 2007 by Melissa Schroeder
Print ISBN: 1-59998-559-4
Digital ISBN: 1-59998-466-0

Editing by Sasha Knight
Cover by Scott Carpenter

First Samhain Publishing, Ltd. electronic publication: May 2007
First Samhain Publishing, Ltd. print publication: November 2007

Dedication

To my parents, Ruth and Steve Bodnar.

Thank you always for your support and love. You can now say the money you spent on my education is being used for more than beating Les at Trivial Pursuit.

Love,

Melissa

Chapter One

January 1808, York

He had to be dead.

Colleen Macgregor dismounted her mare and peered at the gentleman lying flat on his back. Another gust of chilly wind blew drifts of snow across his ashen face.

And a gentleman he was, she thought, noting the workmanship of his clothing. They clung to his skin, outlining the shape of his muscles, leaving little doubt to his size. He wore no coat. Strange, a man with obvious means laid out cold, without a coat, in the middle of her field. And just how the bloody hell had he gotten there?

She looked across the field. No tracks marred the pristine whiteness, but as fast as the snow was falling, it didn't mean he'd been there that long. The snow that had moved in earlier would have covered any tracks, human or otherwise. Colleen glanced back down at the man.

As she studied his facial features more closely, her spectacles slipped down her nose, and she pushed them back up with her gloved hand. She squinted. *Goodness gracious!* His lips were turning blue.

"Sir." She nudged his leg with her foot. He groaned, and she jumped at the sound. "Sir?"

"Mumaphmph." She leaned down closer, and he coughed, his breath billowing in a misty cloud. The stale scent of whiskey she remembered smelling on her stepfather wafted up, and she straightened. A drunk.

She nudged him again, not so gently this time.

"Beatrice, honey, get back in bed," he mumbled. He reached out, as if looking for a pillow, and not finding one, rolled over. Colleen gasped, jumped back and watched him roll into the ditch. He lay face down in the snow unmoving. After a few seconds, the man began to snore.

Snoring, passed out in a ditch. *Good place for a drunk.*

She looked toward her house, then across the field again. The snow was so heavy she could barely make out the path she'd taken from the village. Her companion Gerty would not be able to make it back from her brother's house in this. Colleen didn't fancy the idea of being alone with a strange man, especially with the chance that she wouldn't see anyone for days.

No one. Not one person would trek out in this weather. She knew for a fact none of her neighbors would be able to help the man, since the closest was a good twenty-minute walk away. She'd bid the vicar and his wife, Mrs. Temple, goodbye before picking up a few supplies and making her journey home some thirty minutes earlier. The storm blowing through her village would keep the area deserted for days.

The wind picked up speed, pulling on the unmanageable locks that had escaped her bun. Snowflakes wet her face. She shivered as the dampness sank into her. She looked down at the man again. There was no way he would survive the night. Rotten drunk.

It shamed her that she wanted to leave him to his destiny. Her conscience wouldn't allow it. She knew if she left him, he would die in that ditch. And even though he may deserve it—and she wouldn't doubt he did deserve it—she would not sink to that level. Truthfully, the guilt of leaving him to die, even if he was a rotten stinking drunkard, would eat away at her.

Eyeing her cottage, she made her decision. She would never forgive herself if he froze to death there on her property when she could have possibly prevented it. She didn't have much space but she'd forego her bed for him, she thought, frowning. It was going to be a cold, uncomfortable night.

Before she could change her mind, she mounted her horse and rode to her home. She hooked Bessy up to her dilapidated wagon, the one she used only in emergencies, and hurried back to save the intoxicated stranger.

CRCBCR

Someone who smelled wonderful was carrying him, or trying to carry him. Sebastian Ware's arm was draped over a shoulder of an individual whose stature was considerably less than his. Silky, wet strands of hair clung to his face so he knew his angel was of the female variety. Or a short man with extremely long hair who smelled like a woman.

He took another sniff. Something very comforting. Not Beatrice, the buxom widow he met his first day in York at Freddy's house party. Beatrice tended to gravitate to perfume that reminded him of his mother's gardens. And not his sister, she usually smelled of roses.

No, this scent reminded him of sneaking into the kitchen as a young lad, stealing the first sticky buns Cook had pulled from the oven. Cinnamon. That's what she smelled like. And vanilla. Maybe Cook was helping him up the back stairs so he wouldn't embarrass his mother once again.

"Come on, you drunken sod," the female barked.

She didn't have the strong Welsh accent of Cook but upper-crust English. And she wasn't nice.

"Listen, if you can't help at least a little, I'm dropping you back in the ditch where I found you."

Impertinent hussy.

"Lissen here, you," he said, his tongue as thick as his mother's favorite Persian rug. "I'm in line to an earldom. I am a lord."

The female snorted. "Yes, I just bet you are, Lord of the Drunks. My own mother was married to one of them."

She stopped dragging him, and he finally found the strength to lift his head. Streaks of pain radiated from the back of his skull. Bright white lights burst in front of his eyes.

"Now," she said, apparently unaware his head had exploded, "all we have to do is get you up these steps. I don't want any bellyaching. It's bad enough I'll sleep in a chair tonight so you can have my bed." She sighed, and then added, just loud enough for him to hear, "I should just let you sleep on the floor like a dog."

He turned his head to look at the sharp-tongued hoyden, but the motion left him dizzy, and his stomach revolted. Dropping his head again, he decided vomiting on the woman would not be in his best interest.

Colleen dumped the man on her bed with a thud. Her back ached and her head pounded. She took a few deep breaths attempting to regain her strength. She'd never tried to drag a full-grown, drunken man through the snow before, and this one had lost consciousness halfway to the room.

She studied the lush she'd rescued from certain death and realized he was actually very attractive, if she ignored his blue lips and red nose. His clothing had been made from very fine cloth and had been tailored to fit his lean, hard body. He definitely had money. Or he'd *had* money at one time. Harry, her now deceased stepfather, always had money. He just never held on to it longer than it took him to get to a pub.

Bending at the waist, she picked up his feet and lifted them onto the bed. She would have to get him out of those wet clothes.

First, she pulled off one Hessian. As she lifted his other foot, he chuckled. Not a normal chuckle, but a devilish, stop-her-heart kind of chuckle. She shuddered as her stomach flip-flopped at the completely masculine sound. Grimacing, she dismissed her reaction, blaming it on her damp clothing.

Focusing her attention on his face, she took hold of his other boot. The moment she touched him, his lips curved, bringing out the dimple on the side of his cheek. Ignoring her nerves that had started to dance, she dropped the second boot beside the other on the floor, walked to the side of the bed and began to unbutton his shirt. She leaned over him to complete the task when she felt his hand on her bottom. Every muscle in her body froze. She glanced at his face to witness the same stupid, sloppy smile as he had worn earlier. A flush of heat rushed through her as his hand caressed her skin through the wet fabric of her dress.

Gathering her wits, she stepped away from him and almost laughed at the frown that instantly marred his beautiful face. He looked like a toddler who had been denied a treat. It shouldn't have been funny, considering she usually condemned such behavior. Once she had his shirt undone, she slowly pulled it from his arms. It was not an easy job as Lord King of the Drunks was a world-class grabber with three sets of hands.

11

When she finally completed the task, she dropped the fine linen shirt beside his boots.

She studied the man and wondered how she was going to get those pants off him. If she was smart, and she was, she would clobber him on the head just to get him to pass completely out. Knowing her luck, he would die from the blow, and she would have to explain why she had a half-naked dead man in her bedroom.

He was tall, probably over six feet. The one time he had stood straight, the top of her head reached his chin. Uncommon for her because she usually looked men in the eye. His hair was dark as midnight with a bit of a wave. His skin had a touch of bronze to it, making her think he had not been in this area of the country for long. His nose might have been straight at one time, but it appeared to have been broken recently. A bit of whiskers shadowed his jaw, contributing to his thoroughly disreputable look.

She glanced at his chest. Heat rushed to her face as her pulse increased. In all her twenty-five years, Colleen had never seen a man without a shirt before. She was certain the man lying on her bed was not an average drunk.

If he were, the stranger was in better shape than she suspected Harry had ever been. Lean, not thin, with hardened muscles beneath his golden flesh. He moved and she stood mesmerized by the ripple of muscle.

Licking her lips, she ordered herself to move her attention from his broad shoulders, but only got so far as his nipples, taut from the cold. She shivered as hers tightened in response. Suppressing the urge to cross her arms over her breasts, she shook off her reaction. If she didn't keep her mind on her task, she would never finish.

She looked past his chest to his hardened stomach, bisected by a thin line of black hair that disappeared beneath his breeches. Taking a fortifying breath, she grabbed his trousers and undid them. He chuckled again, a deep, rich sound that sent shivers coursing down her spine. She froze the moment she heard him speak.

"Now, Beatrice, you naughty, naughty wench, there'll be time for that later."

The tone of his voice was at once teasing, flirtatious and completely seductive. Looking up at him, she saw his lips twist, but his eyes remained closed. She released her breath. *Dreaming.* The lout was dreaming about the same hussy he had been talking about earlier.

She took hold of the top of his trousers to pull them down. The material, soaking wet and cold, stuck to his skin. She tried working it down, inch by inch. At the rate she was going, it would take her until April to get the buggers off.

Aggravated, she let go and walked away from the bed. She paced in front of her window, biting on her thumbnail, and decided there was only one way to get the things off him. Well, two, but she didn't feel like wielding a pair of scissors near him, especially not in his delirious state. She stomped to the foot of the bed, grabbed hold of the end of each leg of his pants and tugged with all her might.

Slowly, the material slid off as she continued her efforts. The more she tugged the more they stuck to his skin. But, determined to get him out of the wet clothing, she persisted. When she had them around his ankles, she yanked with a strength she didn't know she possessed, sliding the fabric free of his legs. She lost her balance and fell on her bottom, holding the trousers in her hands.

Still sitting on the floor, she decided to invade the man's privacy and look through his pockets. She felt a spark of guilt, but pushed it aside. Other than a pocket watch, she found nothing. The watch itself spoke of his station in life. Gold, with intricate scrollwork, it was inscribed "To my son, Love, Mother".

She placed the pocket watch on her bedside table and dropped the pants to the floor. Thank goodness he was wearing drawers, although they were almost transparent from being wet. Grabbing her mother's favorite quilt from the rocking chair, she hurried over to cover him and tried not to glance lower than his face. She pulled the quilt up to his neck doubting that when her mother had bought the quilt she envisioned such a rake lying beneath the sunny yellow daises embroidered on it.

"There's a good girl, Mary. Now don't tell Mother about Winifred."

Beatrice, Winifred, Mary? Good Lord, the man had a whole harem of women. And every one of them most likely was happy to get the minimal attention he gave them.

She would never understand the attraction of a charmer. Her mother, God rest her soul, fell for Harry Philpot, a seducer and a drunk, after she had spent three years as a lonely widow.

Looking at Lord Drunk, she knew he was a charmer. His inky hair curled over his forehead, giving him an almost boyish look. She had yet to see his eyes, but given his dark hair and the thick black lashes, she assumed they were brown. She noticed his skin had turned a shade lighter, losing some of its golden hue. Her room had yet to warm up, so she grabbed another quilt from her chest and covered him.

"Thank you, love," he mumbled.

She rolled her eyes. Always the rogue, even when sleeping off an overindulgence. After ensuring he was asleep this time, she rushed outside to get Bessy settled and fed. When she returned, she discovered her own clothes were as wet as the stranger's. If she didn't get out of them soon she might end up ill, and that would do her patient no service.

Colleen chose her navy blue woolen dress. It wasn't fashionable. Well, most of her clothes weren't that fashionable, but this gown was her warmest one, and with a night she knew would be spent up watching the stranger, she wanted something comfortable and warm.

Turning her back to the bed, she began to undress. Her fingers stilled the moment she heard Lord Drunk's chuckle. She glanced behind her, the bodice of her dress sliding off her shoulders. Her heart bounced against her breast but as she studied his face, she saw no sign he was awake. Still, he could rouse at any moment, so she gathered her dress and hurried out of the room.

She returned a few minutes later, dressed and warm. She'd brought another quilt and placed it on top of him. Colleen sighed, knowing she needed to get her food stored and the fire going since the cottage was almost as cold as outside. She finished up her chores, her body aching from the task of hauling wood—not to mention her new occupant. She stepped inside her room and found Lord Drunk sitting up in bed, the quilts draped across his waist.

The soft scrape of her shoe against the floor drew his attention. He pinned her with a pair of icy blue eyes. Tiny fingers of fear prickled over her flesh as she stood frozen.

"Who the hell are you, and where are my bloody clothes?"

Sebastian Ware studied the woman and inwardly grimaced at her expression. She looked as if she were ready to faint. He hadn't meant to sound so mean and surly. The tone of his voice had her backing up a step and he regretted his rash question.

She had spinster written all over her. She wore a morbid woolen dress, faded from many washings and buttoned up to her chin. Her bright red hair had been pulled back in a bun so tight her head probably throbbed. To complete the look, tiny spectacles perched on the bridge of her freckled nose and a cap sat upon her head.

"Lord Dr...er...sir, I'm Colleen Macgregor." Warily, she approached him but stopped a few feet short, looking at him as if he would pounce on her at any moment.

He had awakened a few minutes earlier to find himself stripped out of his clothes and with one hell of a headache. Although he liked a good brandy, he reeked of cheap whiskey, a drink that more often than not made him sick. He had no idea where he was. It was not an odd occurrence for him to wake up in a woman's bed, but he usually remembered her face. Apparently, this woman had something to do with the removal of his clothes.

"Well, Miss—and I presume it is Miss Macgregor—I repeat, where are my bloody clothes?"

She visibly swallowed, and her grey eyes widened behind her lenses. As she took another step back, she reached out in front of her with her hands, as if looking for something—or someone—to protect herself with. After a moment's hesitation she said, "I-I found you outside. Passed out in the snow." She swallowed again.

He studied her and realized she just might be telling the truth. From the innocent expression to the ugly blue dress she wore, she had do-gooder written all over her. He shook his head and another shard of pain shot through it. Closing his eyes, he tried to block out the ache as the room around him spun.

"Oh, sir, you need to lie down."

Now there was an understatement. The way his head felt, he would gladly lie comatose for several days. Slowly, trying to minimize the pain in his skull, he heeded her advice and lay back down.

"Are you warm enough, sir?"

"Yes." Burning up in fact.

Her footsteps neared the bed, and after a moment she pulled the quilts up over his chest again. "Now that that's settled, who are you?"

"Sebastian Ware."

"Visiting from London, are we?" she asked, a bit of sarcasm seeping into her tone. He was happy that she was at least no longer afraid of him.

"Yes. I assume you live in this godforsaken area, but *I* am visiting."

"Hmm, well I don't know what it's like in London, but it's generally not a good idea to drink and pass out in the middle of a blizzard."

He opened his eyes. She stood by the side of the bed, her hands on her hips. The expression on her face reminded him of a reprimanding nanny.

"I didn't drink. I remember a woman...some woman."

"Beatrice?"

For a moment, the offering of Beatrice's name didn't register. When it did, suspicion burned within him. Perhaps she wasn't all she seemed to be. After all, spinsters usually didn't strip men and put them in their beds. The smirk that had been on her face faded and the wariness was back.

"Yes, Beatrice, how did you know?" he asked.

She hesitated, then offered, "You said her name several times."

He still doubted her word, but with his head spinning and his body aching, he needed time to think. To plan.

"Oh, well, yes. I was at Freddy's party, met Beatrice, then..." He tried to grasp at bits of his memory but there was nothing substantial for his mind to grab hold of. He could remember the party, but past that, everything seemed to fade into oblivion. "I can't remember one bloody thing."

"Yes, well, that happens when you drink too much."

"I had nothing to drink, save a solitary glass of brandy," he said from behind clenched teeth. He sat up, prepared to verbally bash the woman, when the streaks of pain shot through his head. There was a bright light and then nothing at all.

CRCBCR

Colleen stared down at Sebastian Ware. Something else was wrong. Drunks passed out, but they definitely did not recover as fast as this one and they did not faint. Eighteen months with her stepfather Harry and she knew what inebriated men did.

She poked him in the arm with her finger and, realizing he truly had fainted, placed her hands on either side of his head. She studied his face and noticed he had regained his color. That was a good sign. It showed that his blood was pumping. She straightened back up and wondered about Mr. Ware. Lord something or other, if his haughty accent and clothes were any indication of his background.

Leaning over him again, she noticed a red stain on her pillow. Gently, she cupped the back of his head, lifted it and found drops of blood marring the ivory linen. She turned his head and gasped when she found more dried blood matted in his hair.

Chapter Two

Colleen leaned closer. Mr. Sebastian Ware had definitely been coshed on the head by something or someone. Or, he could have hit his head the first time he passed out, she supposed.

She straightened and placed a hand on each hip. As she looked down at him, she wondered how she missed the blood to begin with. Thinking back, she closed her eyes, remembering how she found him. If her memory served her right, the snow had been untouched, except for the impression his body had left. Blood would have easily shown up against the whiteness of the snow. Which meant that he'd probably been injured somewhere else and then was either dumped by someone or staggered to where he'd lain.

Not knowing how long he'd had the injury, she assumed it needed cleaning. With all her other troubles, it wouldn't due to have him succumb to an infection.

Noting his even breathing, she left the room quickly. She gathered cloth, sewing supplies, brandy to clean the wound as her mother had taught her and a bowl for the brandy.

She set her supplies on the bedside table then sat down slowly, trying her best not to jostle him. After pouring a bit of brandy into the bowl, she dipped her linen cloth, soaking it in the liquor. With her other hand she gently threaded her fingers through his raven-colored hair, which was unfashionably long and in need of a good trim. He had quite a bit of blood caked in his hair, making it more difficult to find the wound. When she finally did, she discovered a huge bump with a gash in the center.

"Sir? Mr. Ware?" No response. "Mr. Ware?" Still nothing. "Sebastian?"

"Wha..."

"Mr. Ware, you have a nasty cut on the back of your head, and I need to clean it. It's going to sting."

"Cut...sting..." His voice was muffled against the mattress, his tone barely coherent.

She decided it shouldn't wait. Gently, she dabbed the cut, once, twice, then pressed against it.

"Hmm—mumph—bloody hell!" He tried to jerk his head out of her reach, but she held on to it.

"Oh, hush."

He continued to struggle but she tightened her hold. When he apparently realized she wasn't going to let go, he stopped.

"Good God, woman. What are you doing to my head?"

"Cleaning it as I told you." She dabbed at his head with the cloth, trying to clean away the dried blood. "Someone must have been pretty upset with you. You have a good-size knot on the back of your head. And if you don't quiet down, I'm going to give you a matching one right on top of it."

"Why do I have to be quiet?" Knowing he was probably wearing the same disgruntled look as he had earlier, she smiled.

"Because, I don't want to listen to you screaming like a little girl."

"I don't scream like a girl. Ouch! I think you're enjoying this."

She chuckled. "I'm thinking you may not have been that drunk."

"I had only a brandy last night."

"Your clothes reeked of whiskey."

"Hate whiskey," he muttered, sounding like a little boy again.

"Well, you could probably do with a few stitches, but I'm afraid you'll cry."

"Oh, stop. If I need a few stitches, I'll take it. Stiff upper lip and all that."

She chuckled again, and Sebastian resisted joining in. He had pegged her for a prude. Truth be told, he knew she was. Though if he hadn't seen that morbid dress and scraped back hair, he would have never known.

More than likely it was her voice. Low, husky and comforting, it was the type of voice a man liked to hear in the bedroom. The sound of it sent a rush of heat to his belly. The contradiction between her voice and her personality confused him, and also intrigued him. He willed the feeling away. Spinsters were not his cup of tea, no matter how sensual they sounded.

"Now, I'm going to stitch it up." Her tone was so kind and reassuring, he wondered if she were the same woman who had threatened to give him another bump on the head.

"You thought I was a drunk," he said, wincing as she began stitching up his wound.

"I did find you lying lifeless in the snow, with no coat and smelling of cheap whiskey. What was I to think?" Her voice was no longer as warm, but practical instead.

"You know Beatrice?"

She remained silent but he did not want to let it go.

"Miss Macgregor?"

"No. You mentioned her once or twice." Her voice had cooled a bit more, and he realized he must have said something to embarrass her. With his past, that could be just about anything.

"Hmm...any other interesting tidbits I shared I should know about?"

"No, you just mentioned a few names." He could hear the shrug in her voice.

"Names?"

She hesitated, then said, "Female names."

"Oh?" When she continued on with her task and ignored his prodding, irritation inched up his spine, making his head pound harder. "I didn't try anything, did I?"

She cleared her throat. "N...no. Not really. There you go. All done."

Miss Macgregor stood, and Sebastian rolled over on his back, being careful of his head.

He studied her as she gathered her supplies. "So you saw no one around when you found me?"

She placed all the items in a basket and answered him without looking in his direction. "No. And I daresay you were there for a time." Picking up the basket, she turned to him.

He watched her for a second or two, trying to make eye contact, but she looked everywhere but at him.

"Why?"

Finally, she brought her gaze back to his face. "Why what?"

"Why did you think that I had been there for a long time?"

Relief relaxed her features. "You were covered in snow. Less than an hour though, because I would have noticed you when I left to go to visit the vicar and his wife." She walked toward the door, then stopped when she reached it and turned around. "I'm going to put these away. Are you hungry?"

His stomach rumbled, and her lips curved into a small smile. Her grey eyes sparkled behind her spectacles. For just a second, she didn't look so much like a spinster.

"I'll take that as a yes. I'll be back in a few minutes. I have something for the pain, but I'm not sure if you should take anything just yet. Head injuries are tricky. Rest while I'm gone."

With the click of the door, Sebastian relaxed. He had been on edge since he had awakened and found himself practically naked and in a strange place. It wasn't as if it hadn't happened before, but he usually remembered how he got there, and felt a damn sight better since a warm body frequently accompanied him in bed.

At least the lady didn't seem to be ready to throw him out. He glanced at the door again, wondering about his savior. No young woman of his acquaintance would have hauled a complete stranger to her cottage and fixed the injury. Well, Anna, his sister, probably would, but she rarely used good sense. And she would have fainted at the first sight of blood.

He examined his surroundings and realized her furnishings were of quality. Not the highest, and much of it outdated, but definitely more than one would expect of a young lady who apparently lived by herself in a tiny home. Small glass and ceramic figurines littered the surface of a beautifully crafted cherrywood dresser. Much nicer than he'd expected of a woman who dressed in such atrociously ugly clothes.

There was a strange combination of English and a hint of something else—Scottish?—in her voice. She also spoke with a sense of decorum, a sense of culture one usually heard from aristocracy. He chuckled at the thought of Miss Knickers-in-a-bind being a member of the aristocracy, spending her time hauling drunks in from out of the cold.

Gingerly, he lifted his head and carefully tested her stitches. What the hell had he been doing to end up passed out in the snow, smelling of whiskey?

CR CB CR

Colleen rushed her preparation of the evening meal. Since she had left so early that morning, she hadn't made bread. She looked out the window and noticed the snow getting heavier. Knowing that there was a good chance they would be snowed in for at least a day or two, she pulled out all the ingredients to make bread and began her task. The weather, coupled with the fact she needed to keep an eye on Mr. Ware, made her anxious to finish. At the thought of her patient, a delicious thrill shot through her, warming her from the inside out. Her hands stilled in the bread dough as her mind froze.

What was she thinking? She was *not* thrilled to be spending her afternoon with a totally unrepentant rake with dark blue eyes and a dimple. Colleen didn't even like men that much, especially charmers. Except for her father, she had not met a man worth the trouble. From the drunk her mother married to her sister's lover, a powerful aristocrat with a nasty temper, Colleen had good reason to avoid men.

She shook herself from her morbid thoughts and hurried through her chores. In her opinion, she was better off knowing most men were not like her father. Most men were drunks and cheats and rakes. Not unlike the man in her bed at the moment. She'd do well to remember that, especially when his smile did funny things to her insides.

CRCBCR

Not twenty minutes later, Colleen breezed through the door to her room with a tray of tea and sandwiches in her hands.

"It took you long enough."

The withering look she gave him did not help his dangerous mood.

"I can leave you to starve," she said, her tone sickly sweet.

"I'll just follow you dressed only in my drawers."

It delighted him when her face flushed with mortification. He was even more pleased when she refused to back down. "Listen, Lord Ware, I saved your life. You owe me."

He winced and she smiled—a bit evilly.

"You know it and I know it. Besides"—she shrugged— "you'd never make it to the door in your condition."

Sharp-tongued spinster. Sebastian would love to tell the woman just whom she was dealing with. He could ruin her in a heartbeat. But, the truth was, he didn't have much choice. The woman had taken him into her home, at a risk to her reputation, and he owed her a boon. No matter how much it irritated him, Wares did not leave a good deed unrewarded. And besides, she was right. He really didn't think he would make it very far on his own two feet. If he could regain them to begin with.

"What do you plan to do with me?"

She turned an adorable shade of pink and busied herself with setting the tray on the bedside table. So Miss Macgregor was not immune to him after all. Why a curl of heat warmed the pit of his stomach he did not know, but the very proper Miss Macgregor's blush caused a certain part of his anatomy to sit up and take notice. He pulled his knee up to hide his reaction from her. Lord knew she'd probably go running from the room screaming. It was scary enough to him, he could only imagine her response.

He settled back against the pillows, his head throbbing now. He tried to ignore the ache but it radiated from the area she had worked on and sent fingers of pain coursing through his head.

"I really don't know. The storm is getting worse by the minute so you may be stuck here for a few days."

"A few days? I'd planned to return to London tomorrow."

"I do not think that is going to happen." She offered him a frown but applied herself to making their refreshments. "Do you take anything in your tea?"

He shook his head and it sent the room whirling. The wave of nausea took him by surprise and almost had him embarrassing himself by vomiting. Maybe he had lost more blood than he thought.

She poured the tea into a cup. The tiny cup matched the teapot that sat on a silver service. While not new, the whole service was well cared for. Sebastian still could not piece together the puzzle that was Miss Macgregor. She offered him his cup then poured one for herself. She placed a few sandwiches on a plate and handed it to him.

He took a bite and was pleasantly surprised. "Meat!"

She chuckled, and he looked at her, one eyebrow raised. She shrugged. "Men like meat. Although, I was worried you would be sick from that bump on the head. I didn't want you humiliating yourself by vomiting."

He ignored her barb and said, "You seem to know a lot about men."

Her smile faded. "What do you mean by that?" The sharp tone in her voice was back, and he was relieved. If she sounded like that, maybe he could control these insane reactions he had to her.

"I mean you seem to know a lot about their likes and dislikes."

"I had a father and a stepfather."

"Oh." He took another bite. "Well, I need to get down to the nearest town and hire a horse."

Her grey eyes narrowed. "Apparently you weren't listening, sir. There's a blizzard raging outside. There will be no horses to hire, no one to help. From my experience, and I talk of twenty-five years of experience, this storm may end soon, but the effects of it will be felt for days. I know for a fact that the inn is filled with stranded travelers. There is no way to get out of the area for at least a day or two. Even for Lord King of the Drunks, second in line to an earldom."

"Quit calling me that." Wariness whipped through him. Maybe she did know him. Maybe he'd been a mark, someone she decided to steal from. "How do you know about the earldom?"

"You told me when you were reprimanding me for not being nice."

"Oh." He sneezed, surprised at the chill that left him shivering.

"I was afraid of that," she said, her voice stern with reproof. Like it had been his fault he'd caught cold. She placed her teacup down and laid the back of her hand on his forehead. Her hand was cool against his warm skin. And he was hot, burning up. He had not realized just how hot until he felt her hand on his skin.

"You're going to be miserable when that cold sets full in." She crossed her arms beneath her breasts. Worry knit her brow.

"Well," he said and shivered, "I'm not going to get well sitting here naked."

Her face flamed again. "You are not naked." She stared at him for a moment or two. "I'm going to the attic, I believe, perhaps, you will fit into some of my father's things. It's been thirteen years, but I think you are of the same height, although I may be remembering wrong. Of course, they're a decade out of style, but I'm sure you'll survive." She walked to the end of the bed and opened a chest, pulling out another quilt. "Here you go." While she piled it on top of the three other quilts, she had to lean over him, and the scent of cinnamon reached him again.

"Cinnamon," he said, his eyes suddenly heavy. "You smell like sticky buns."

"You get well, and I'll make you some. I'll get you dry clothes."

She felt his forehead once again and sighed. Comfort that he had not felt since childhood wrapped around him, and he drifted into sleep.

C511C5511CR

Colleen closed the attic door behind her then surveyed the room. It was a long rectangular room with only two small windows, one that looked out on the front of the house and one for the back. A multitude of old toys from her and her sister's youth littered the room, along with rarely used pieces of furniture. Several trunks of clothes were stored up here, most of them her mother's clothes from her coming out.

Jane Macgregor had allowed her daughters a childhood free of the duty to marry based on social standing and the etiquette she said almost choked her. They had been taught proper manners, but her mother believed that childhood should be unencumbered of obligations to the family.

Instead, Colleen and her younger sister, Deidre, spent many cold afternoons such as this one, dressing up and pretending to be princesses at a ball. The attic had been a world of their own creation, spun in golden dreams of what they thought adulthood in the ton would be like, never understanding what living that kind of life meant. They spent hours in the attic recreating their fantasy. Balls, teas, even visits to the King of England had been on their events list.

She breathed in the stale, musty air. Some months had passed since she had rummaged through the trunks, but that day had been warm and she had opened the window for fresh air. She glanced at the small square window, plastered with snow and ice, and decided that would be out of the question. Her eyes searched the room for the trunk that held her father's clothes. She spied it in the corner behind a broken chair. She set her lantern on a table, testing it first to make sure it was able to hold her one source for light without falling apart.

After she moved the chair out of the way, she lifted the top of the trunk and knelt down to look inside. Neatly folded and packed tight, her father's clothes sat within the trunk. She remembered her mother, Deidre and herself packing them away and crying over the fact that William Macgregor was gone from their lives. As Colleen shifted through the clothes, the familiar scent of her father's pipe tobacco intermingled with must.

Even after all these years, that smell brought to mind sitting on her father's lap as he read a story to her and her sister. Her father had been a strong, silent man, with a hearty laugh and a soft heart. He'd always had time for his daughters and wife, and when he died, it was as if the family had lost its soul. She sniffled and tears prickled her eyes, either from the bittersweet memories or the dust, she wasn't sure.

After pulling out several white linen shirts and a couple of pairs of trousers, she began searching for a nightshirt. Certainly, her father had one of those. She emptied the trunk and still found nothing so she repacked the clothes she did not need and closed the trunk. Glancing around the room again, she could not think of another place her mother may have stored any clothes. The other trunks were filled with her mother's and Deidre's clothes. She knew because she had packed them. Surely her father had slept in some form of clothing, but what?

The memory of Sebastian Ware in his transparent drawers flashed through her mind, and her face heated. Good night, what was she thinking about him for? It was completely improper and she didn't even like men with his personality. But it was hard to resist his charm, because, even injured and wet, he was a fine specimen of a man. Before she had covered him with a quilt, she had glimpsed his golden skin and lean muscular legs, and just thinking about it made her pulse quicken. She was sure if she had concentrated hard enough, she would have been able to see his nether regions through the material.

Mortification sent another rush of blood to her face. What was wrong with her? She had never even thought anything about a man in that manner before. He was attractive, but other than he seemed to have had a string of women in his bed, she knew little else.

She picked up her father's clothes and headed toward the door before any other improper thoughts assaulted her.

CRCBCR

Quietly, as not to disturb Lord Ware, Colleen crept into the room. He lay in the bed, shivering under the four quilts. She shut the door and hurried over, dropping the clothes on the foot of the bed.

He really didn't look like such a rake when he lay sleeping. A lock of hair curled over his forehead, his features relaxed in slumber, making him look years younger. She was concerned about his fever. Her worry intensified when she placed her hand on his forehead once again. Heat rolled off him, and his shivering increased.

"Mr. Ware? Mr. Ware, I have some clothes for you." He stirred, moving his legs about and thrashing his head from side to side. "Lord Ware...S-Sebastian, we need to get some clothes on you."

In an instant, his hand whipped out, snaked around her neck and drew her onto the bed. He rolled over, and she found herself trapped beneath a practically naked man.

Chapter Three

Sebastian's eyes never opened as he bent his head and touched his lips to hers. At first, Colleen didn't react. She couldn't. One moment she was standing, the next she was flat on the bed, Sebastian's hot body on top of hers. She still wasn't sure how that had happened in the first place.

He slid both of his hands up to cup her face, stroking his thumbs across her cheeks as his lips plied hers with tender kisses. Her heart fluttered then picked up pace. Her head started to spin because she'd only been kissed once before in her life. If Tommy Martin had kissed her as well as Sebastian, she would have never given him that black eye.

The bruising kiss Tommy had bestowed upon her had lacked passion of any kind. This was nothing like that.

Sebastian brushed his mouth over hers. His tongue traced the seam of her closed lips. The sensation was foreign—almost frightening. Nothing had prepared her for the yearning of his touch. His fingers still stroked her cheeks. His mouth still caressed her lips.

When she felt his tongue again, the simple touch sent her senses reeling. Her breasts swelled, her nipples tightened against his chest. She gasped at her body's reaction. He used the opportunity to delve inside her mouth. Heat seeped from him, warming her, relaxing her. He pulled away from her, his lips hovering, his breath on her face, his eyes closed.

"Come on, love, just one little kiss." His voice was deeper than before, and the sound of it danced along her nerve endings.

She couldn't help the warmth curling in her belly, or the acceleration of her pulse. When he bent his head this time, she threw caution to the wind, closed her eyes and joined him in the kiss.

It was so delicious, so wicked, so incredibly *wet.*

She opened her mouth again, and his tongue slipped inside, sending a tidal wave of heat racing through her. She slid her hands around his neck and toyed with the ends of his hair. One hand eased down her throat, caressing her neck, her collarbone, then his fingers brushed against her aching breast. At first, the strokes were feather light. Once, twice, the tips of his fingers glided across her nipple and even through the woolen material of her dress, the sensation of the soft touches further puckered her nipple.

His hand closed around her breast, and a surge of energy filled her body. Her heart beat violently against her chest. The tantalizing warmth in her stomach dropped and tumbled to her loins as he slid one of his legs between hers, then the other, situating his lower body between her outstretched legs, his private areas touching hers. He ground his groin intimately against her, and even through her dress she could feel the heat of him, the long, hard length of his arousal.

He skimmed both of his hands to her waist, and before she knew what he was about, the skirt of her dress and her petticoats were drawn to her waist, his hands on her bottom as he pulled her tightly to him.

Liquid heat poured through her, clouding her senses. His lips left hers as he kissed a path along her jaw, his tongue branding her skin. As he continued to rub the hard length of his erection against her, pressure built in that exact spot where they touched. Her body quivered, preparing for something she still did not comprehend. She didn't know, could not fathom what she needed, but knew that Sebastian could deliver the relief she sought.

Even as it frightened her, Colleen could not dismiss the excitement coursing in her body. Sebastian quickened his movements. What Colleen did not understand, her body did and matched his rhythm, urging her to reach a pinnacle.

Sparks shot through her as his teeth nipped at her earlobe. She moved her hands from around his neck to the hard length of his muscled back. He dropped his head to her shoulder, and she waited—waited for him to continue the delicious assault. His breath was hot against her neck.

Seconds clicked by, but nothing happened. She opened her eyes only to find her glasses had fogged over. Blinking, she waited for them to clear, then Sebastian's hands relaxed on her bottom. He was no longer moving. She pushed at his shoulder but he did not respond. Then she heard a suspicious snuffle. He was snoring. She lay beneath him, waiting for him to finish his seduction, and he had fallen asleep.

Reality crashed down around her. The man was fevered, half out of his mind. She had allowed him to kiss her. Not only kiss her, but grind against her, caress her, turn her into some kind of a hussy.

Her face burned with embarrassment and shame as she placed her hands on his shoulders and pushed. He didn't move, only tightened his arms around her waist, his fingers still warm on her bottom, and mumbled something she couldn't make out.

"Lord Ware?" she whispered.

Nothing. She wiggled her body, and his arms loosened. He was so heavy she didn't know if she could get out from beneath him. Funny how his weight didn't seem to bother her when she was writhing beneath him like some loose woman.

She took a breath, and with all the strength she had, shoved his shoulders. He rolled off her and thankfully stayed on the bed. She jumped up and scooted to the other side of the room, placing as much distance as possible between her and the wicked man. Her lips still tingled. How could she, the woman who frightened most of the men in the village so that no one dared approach her, turn shamelessly wanton because of just one kiss?

She lifted her fingers to her swollen lips and glanced at her reflection in the mirror. Her hair was disheveled, half of it fallen from the topknot. There were red marks along her jawline where his whiskers had scratched her. Her breathing was finally returning to normal, but her eyes were still overbright.

Good night. She looked like her sister did when her mother had caught Michael O'Hearney stealing kisses. Her eyes narrowed, and she looked back at the blackguard responsible for the embarrassment.

He shivered, and she realized she had left a sick man uncovered. Slowly, she approached the bed. When she had shoved him off her, he had rolled over onto the quilts. Carefully, she kept one eye on him as she worked the quilts from beneath him. A smile curved his lips, showing a hint of dimple, and then his face relaxed once again. So innocent and so deadly at the same time.

CRCBCR

Colleen sighed as she carried the tray of food to her room. She'd had a long day getting ready for the storm, running into the village for supplies. Now she had a delicious stranger in her bed to worry about.

She stopped in her tracks and shook her head. Thinking of Lord Ware as delicious or delectable or any other kind of edible description was out of the question. Because thinking of him in that manner made her think of his lips. Thinking of his lips made her think of his kisses and that was just not a good idea.

She needed to forget that her whole body felt as if it would explode the moment he touched her. Even now heat swept through her at the memory. He was a rake, good at his chosen profession and it had nothing to do with her.

With that self-proclamation, she nodded and continued on her path.

Balancing the tray in one hand, she opened the door. When she spied his eyes closed and his even breathing, she released a breath she hadn't realized she was holding. Thanking her keeper for small miracles, she walked to his bedside. After setting the tray on the table, she looked down at him, not at all encouraged by his shivers.

"Lord Ware, I brought some broth for you." He turned in the direction of her voice but his eyes didn't open. "Sebastian, you need to help me."

She sat on the bed beside him. His face was flushed with fever, his brow damp with perspiration. Along with the broth, she carried in a basin of cool water. She knew to bring down his temperature, she would have to bathe him with the water and pump him full of liquids. She had attempted to do just that after Deidre suffered her miscarriage but had not been successful. This time she would not fail.

ങ്ങങ

"I will be granted a divorce!"

Colleen jerked awake at the sound of an angry male voice. For a brief moment, she was disoriented and almost panicked. The unfamiliarity of waking to the sound of a man caused her heartbeat to quicken as she looked around for help. Then her mind began to function—slowly at first, but it was working.

Straightening in the chair, she glanced over at her patient. His eyes were still closed, and he moved restlessly beneath the bedclothes. Wearily, she moved her head from one side to another, then rolled her shoulders. The past two days had been long, frightening and painful. Keeping watch over Sebastian had taken every bit of energy she had. Through the days and nights, she had listened to his rantings.

At first, she had tried to ignore him, but it had been impossible as he raged against a woman she imagined was his wife.

"There is no way I will be cuckolded. That is not my child."

Pulling herself out of the chair and onto her feet, she stretched, working out the stiffness that had developed. She padded barefoot to the bed. Sebastian tossed and turned, thrashing about.

"You won't stop me. I don't care about the scandal."

Colleen swallowed. She had learned a lot about him the last few days. He was married, or had been at one time. Through his ramblings, she gathered Mrs. Ware had the morals of an alley cat. But then, from what she understood, it was common among the ton to have marriages like that. It was one of the reasons her mother never wanted an arranged marriage.

His shivers were so pronounced she could see him quivering from beneath the mountain of quilts. Worry cramped her stomach. The fear of losing him to a fever brought tears to her eyes. Sniffing, she fought them, not wanting to succumb to feminine hysterics. She was stronger than that. Knowing there was nothing she could do but wait for the fever to break didn't help.

She walked to the window and peered outside at the desolate image of her snow-filled meadow. The snow had continued for two days. She was a little worried about supplies, but now that the storm seemed to be tapering off, she knew the vicar and his wife would be out to check on her. They did not own a sled, but past experience told her they would fret if they didn't see her soon. They might be her only hope, if Sebastian's condition did not improve. She had worried many times during her lonely hours of watching over him.

"I don't believe I've seen a lovelier sight."

She gasped and turned at the sound of his voice. He was still shivering a bit, but a slight smile curved his cracked lips, and his eyes looked clearer than they had in the past two days.

"From the look on your face, I've given you a worry."

"Given me a worry?" she asked when she finally found her voice, which was hoarse with emotion.

His eyes were unclouded, and he seemed to be more alert than he had been in the past forty-eight hours. Relief poured through her and she fought the urge to jump for joy.

"Yes you did. Two days' worth of worry to be exact."

Sebastian closed his eyes for a second, his mind still foggy from his illness. Her voice, softer than the day they met, wrapped around him. When he opened his eyes, he noticed her concerned stare. The comfort she offered warmed him from the inside out. What stroke of fate had brought him to her path?

Sebastian didn't know but he knew that one twist had probably saved his life.

She wore a pristine white wrapper, but she had braided her hair, and it reached her hips. The sight held him momentarily speechless. He would have never guessed the woman had so much hair. All he could think of was running his fingers through it, feeling it tickle his chest...

"Two days... Bloody *hell*."

Her eyes widened behind her spectacles at the blasphemy. Although it irritated him, he should have better manners than that. This woman had rescued him and nursed him through his sickness.

"I apologize. My language... Well, I apologize."

She chuckled, a rich, full chuckle that sent a wave of heat down his spine that had nothing to do with the fever. "Oh, don't worry. Harry had the mouth of a sailor."

A smiled played about her lips as she walked forward and stopped by the side of the bed.

Close enough to grab.

Where the hell had that idea come from? He shook his head trying to clear it.

"Harry?"

"My stepfather."

Good Lord. He glanced toward the door, and she chuckled again, capturing his attention once more.

"He's deceased. There is no worry of being forced to marry me."

"Really? Things like that have been known to happen."

"It won't happen here. And the one thing that almost killed you could save you. The blizzard will keep people away for days. They know I stocked up on supplies and can handle myself."

The forceful tone of her voice had him convinced. She leaned closer and touched the back of her hand to his forehead. Her braid fell forward over her shoulder, the scent of cinnamon drifting around him.

"It seems your fever has finally broken." Her lips pulled down in a frown.

"What's wrong?"

"What? Oh, nothing." She walked toward the door. "I'm going to the kitchen to warm some broth. I haven't gotten much down you."

Two days. He'd forgotten. "I'll need to arrange a horse as soon as possible."

She turned, her hand still resting on the doorknob. "I doubt anyone will be leaving soon. The town inn is probably still locked up tight." Releasing the door, she walked to the window. "It's been snowing the entire time you've been recovering. It finally slowed down, but I doubt anyone is braving the weather just yet. It's still piled fairly deep, and the hard winds are blowing the drifts. Now, I'll get you something to eat. It shouldn't take but a few moments."

Her full red lips curled and something nudged his memory. Somewhere, his mind brought back the tasting of those lips, the touch of her hand at the base of his neck, her full breast against his palm. He shook his head again. The fever must have soured his brain. The woman would have chopped off his hand had he touched her.

"You just rest," she said.

She slipped out the door. Her scent still lingered in the room. He licked his lips, thinking about Cook's sticky buns, and winced at the pain. His lips were as dry as his throat. He massaged his temples. Two days out of his mind with fever. Hopefully, he hadn't said anything incriminating. A slow smile spread across his lips. Maybe he had. Maybe he had shocked her. Served the prude right.

ଔଔଔ

As Colleen set a kettle on the tray, the muted sound of a carriage froze her very action. Who would be here in the middle of the night, in such horrible weather? She peeked out the window and almost cursed. She'd learned quite a few new words while nursing Lord Ware. The vicar descended from the carriage, his already round body fuller from the amount of extra clothing he was wearing. He and one of the stable lads from the inn were walking to her door.

Panic lanced through her. She had to get to Lord Ware and warn him to be quiet.

As she neared the door, she thought about her varied reactions to Lord Ware. While he slept, she had forgotten what a rogue the man was. When he had first awakened a few moments earlier, she had been paralyzed by the memory of their shared kiss, worried that he would tease her. Thankfully, the man had been too sick and appeared to have no memory of the event. And for him to think that she was trying to trap him into marriage by getting caught with him in her room. Blasted man!

She balanced the tray with one hand, opened the door with the other and almost dropped the tray when she saw him. He had pulled himself out of bed and was using the footboard to support himself as he walked. His back was to her, so intent on his task he hadn't heard her.

"Lord Ware!"

At the sound of her voice, he turned, lost his balance and fell to the floor with a curse. She hurried to the nightstand, setting the tray down then helped him to his feet. His face was flushed and a white line around his mouth indicated how much pain he was in.

"What are you doing out of bed?"

"Had to use the chamber pot."

She slung his arm around her shoulders and helped him toward the bed. He leaned on her, and she almost toppled the two of them. She'd forgotten how heavy he was.

"You should have waited for me. You don't want to have the fever return by overexerting yourself." Her voice was sharper than she had meant it to be, but she couldn't help it. His body was hot and so hard, and the whiskers on his cheeks brushed her forehead a couple of times. All she could think of was that kiss. Her whole body tingled from the memory.

He tried to struggle free. His angry movements caused him to lose his balance, and he tumbled on the bed, pulling her with him. She landed on top of him, her head smacking his chin. Placing a hand on each side of his head, she lifted herself. Stars danced in front of her eyes. She opened her mouth to reprimand him, but the sound of footsteps and the creak of the door stopped her.

Chapter Four

For just a moment, Sebastian couldn't react. He held himself immobile, unable to get his mind to function. All of Miss Macgregor's many curves were pressed against him. He could do nothing to stop his body's reaction to the weight of her breasts against his chest.

A flash of memory—flesh molding to flesh, the taste of innocent passion entwined with a seductive whisper—sparked across his mind. Before he could grasp it, it vanished like it had earlier, but his body reacted to it all the same. Raising herself to her hands, she wiggled against his groin and he could feel the very heat of her.

When his head stopped spinning, anger ignited. The little liar! She'd set him up, and he had fallen for it. Drawing in a deep breath, he told himself to not allow the temper threatening to boil over into full-blown rage take hold.

He still couldn't believe she had done it. Miss Macgregor had planned on trapping him and having someone catch them so he would have to marry her. For some unknown reason, hurt twisted with the anger. He didn't understand it, didn't even want to know why. But it was there and it made him even madder.

He looked at her, ready to tell her in no uncertain terms that he would not succumb to her manipulations. But, the sheer panic that flashed in her eyes told him she already knew he would not help her. She struggled off the bed, and it caused the same unbelievable reaction from him. His groin tightened and his blood drained from his head. The woman was a temperamental, uptight, judgmental prude. He had avoided women like her with a passion, mainly because he found them unappealing. Around her, though, he acted as if he were a randy stallion scenting a mare.

She finally gained her feet and her eyes widened when she saw who was at the door. Sebastian followed her horrified gaze to find a rather rotund, short gentleman wrapped in what appeared to be five layers of clothes. The man's mouth dropped open in astonishment, and his eyes rounded in what could only be described as horror.

A young man stood behind him, peering over the gentleman's shoulder to get a better view. A devilish smile curved his lips, making Sebastian even more suspicious.

"Miss Macgregor, I would like to know the meaning of this," the older man said, his voice ripe with condemnation.

The young man chuckled, and the sound of it grated down Sebastian's spine. "Looks to me like we didn't need to worry about ye, Miss Macgregor."

Sebastian shot the young man a threatening look and was happy to see the leer fade from his face. Miss Macgregor was silent for once. He glanced in her direction. She was white as a sheet, her pulse fluttering in her throat. Her tongue darted out to wet her lips. She swallowed nervously, then licked her lips again. Sebastian couldn't help noticing just how much he wanted to taste her.

She cleared her throat twice, breaking his thoughts of mouths and tasting. "Mr. Pearson, John, I would like to introduce Lord Sebastian Ware. Mr. Pearson is the local vicar."

Her voice was threaded with worry. She looked at him as if he were going to announce her as his mistress. Silly chit.

"It's a pleasure. I would stand and greet you properly, but I've been recovering from a head wound."

"So that's what they call it now," John said with a snicker.

Miss Macgregor rushed forward, apparently worried of what these two men thought of her. He wanted to tell her it was a little late for that, and truthfully, why would she worry if she bagged herself a rich man?

"Really, John. Behave yourself!" exclaimed Mr. Pearson.

"Mr. Pearson, it's not what you think," she pleaded.

"Doesn't matter. You need to decide what you are going to do. Wouldn't look good for you to take up with a man."

"I haven't taken up with a man." Her voice had turned as brittle as the northern wind but there was a hint of fright beginning to thread her words. "Lord Ware was injured. I found him on the way home the day the blizzard hit. I couldn't leave him in the snow. He would have died."

Her voice rose, a hint of hysteria invading her tone. Sebastian would normally take comfort in it, even gloat, but the reminder that she possibly saved his life stopped him.

He turned his attention back to Mr. Pearson. The older man was no longer looking at Miss Macgregor, but at him.

"Once word gets out..." The older man let his voice drift off as he cast a knowing glance at John.

Out of the corner of his eye, Sebastian noticed her shoulders slump. Most of his anger faded and the urge to comfort her almost had him pulling himself to his feet and going to her. For some insane reason, he wanted to drag her against him and assure her that all would be well.

Again, a memory prodded of touching her, of feeling her heart beat against his, but it dissolved as he reminded himself of her deception. He might not be as suspicious if she had not assured him earlier. He had one disastrous marriage in his past. The thought of being shackled to another woman, having to go through what he had endured before, did not comfort him. Rage consumed him, threatening to overcome his common sense, but Mr. Pearson's voice interrupted Sebastian's morbid thoughts.

"Mrs. Pearson insisted I come to check on you. I was going to wait until morning, but she just wouldn't let it be. The snow had slowed so I came out here with John to confirm that everything was well. And we find you frolicking with a man." He paused to take a deep breath, his body language not so much showing anger, but resignation. "I don't know what to make of it."

Sebastian may have been annoyed with Miss Macgregor, but he did not like the accusatory manner in which the vicar spoke.

"I would be very careful when you are talking about Miss Macgregor." His voice was deathly calm, icy. Both Mr. Pearson and his younger companion looked surprised. The older man's faded blue eyes studied Sebastian for a moment before turning shrewd.

Colleen released a breath, her aggravation with his interruption apparent. "Lord Ware, there is no reason—"

"I will not have these men slander you in front of me. I just wonder what right these two had, barging into your home."

"We knocked, and then we heard the noise in here. I was worried Miss Macgregor was being attacked." Mr. Pearson offered that bit of information without an ounce of regret.

Sebastian, still seated on the bed, crossed his arms over his chest and studied the vicar. He seemed to be telling the truth. And there was no way these two would have known about him. Colleen had no way of telling others about his presence. Unless she had lied about who had been by while he'd been sick with fever. His attention shifted back to the men. With only two of them as witnesses, they could possibly keep the locals from knowing.

"There is no reason for anyone to know about this."

The silence stretched as the vicar scrutinized Sebastian and then Miss Macgregor. Then he glanced at John. "John, would you leave us for a moment?"

John frowned and looked to argue, but after studying the vicar's stern expression, he shook his head and turned away. He left them, his feet dragging as he walked reluctantly down the hall.

"There is no way John will keep mum about this," the vicar said when they were finally alone. "Nothing I say or do will hold his tongue for long." He glanced at Miss Macgregor. "You know what he is like. He craves attention and will use anything to get it. He might be quiet for a day or two, but that would be the extent of his secret keeping. And at that point, you will be gone, and Miss Macgregor will be forced to fight the condemnation on her own."

Put that way, it did sound pretty bad.

"I think you two have much to discuss. We'll be waiting just outside the door." He shot Sebastian a warning look, his sharp eyes sparking with anger. He left the door open a crack, something that bothered Sebastian to no end.

Sebastian dismissed the vicar and turned his attention to Miss Macgregor. She wouldn't look at him. Her head was bent and she had taken immense interest in her hands clenched before her. She hadn't taken her eyes off them since the vicar left. He couldn't believe they had been caught in such a predicament. Irritation curled in his stomach as the implications became clearer.

"Well, I guess we do have something to discuss." His voice dripped with derision.

His accusation hit a sore spot. She whirled around, her face flushed with anger. "We have nothing to discuss. There is no way I am going to marry the likes of you. I wouldn't lower myself. So you are free."

He stared, nonplussed by the statement. After years of avoiding matchmaking mamas and scheming debutantes, he'd just been spurned by a spinster. A spinster with no prospects and who could very well face condemnation in her own little corner of the world.

Before he could form an opinion on that, she placed a hand on each hip and advanced. "I've never wanted to marry. It makes a woman subservient and gives the man control of her money." She stopped within inches of stepping on his toes. "We have to figure a way out of this!"

"Let me get this straight," he snapped. "You don't want me to do the honorable thing?"

"N-no. I never want to get married, especially to a man like you."

"A man like me! What do you mean a man like me?" His voice had risen, and he fisted his hands on the bed. She slowly backed away, not moving her gaze from his fists. All the color drained from her face, and she bit her lip.

She swallowed. "You don't have to be so angry."

Sebastian stared at the impossible woman. First, she tried to trap him into marriage and then told him she wanted nothing to do with him. Now, she was crowded against the door as if he were going to attack her.

"What the bloody hell are you doing, running out the door? I'm not going to do anything. I can barely stand up."

Her eyes widened behind her frames. As if to calm herself, she took a deep breath and her shoulders relaxed.

"Now, are you trying to tell me this was not a trap?"

She stared at him for a moment. Her mouth opened as if she were about to say something, but instead she started laughing.

Not some little twitter like the debutantes gracing the parlors at Almack's. No this was a big, full belly laugh, her joy bubbling over, filling the room, despite the situation. Even though he was irritated with her, he couldn't stop the way the sound of it sent a rush of heat to his groin. She doubled over, crossing her arms around her midsection, tears streaming down her face.

After a few moments, her laughing eased a bit and he asked, "Now what did I say?"

"You...you think I wanted to trap you into marriage."

"I don't see why that is funny."

Her laughter had finally died, and she wiped the wetness from her face. She looked up at him and started laughing again.

"That is quite enough!" Really, who did the woman think she was? She calmed down, but amusement still danced in her eyes. "I am more than suitable for a woman of your station."

"No."

"Why not?"

A snort of laughter escaped, but she controlled another outburst. "No, and I don't want to marry you."

"Really, what's so wrong with me?"

She grunted. "You're a rake with a harem full of women. You had a bad marriage, and you probably think that all women are like your deceased wife. I'm not interested in being someone's chattel."

All true, but it didn't change the predicament they were in. "A harem full of women... How did you know about my wife?"

She glanced away and then met his gaze. "You talked while you were sick."

Lord only knew what he had said to her while he'd been sick. Apparently, it was enough to make her not want to marry him. She might be opposed to marriage, but marriage to him wasn't a worse prospect than losing her reputation.

"We have to do something."

All humor fled from her face as she sobered instantly. Her eyes lost their twinkle, her posture tensed and her lips turned down in a frown. He almost regretted dashing cold water on her merriment but, bloody hell, he could not let the woman ruin her good name.

"We don't have to do anything. I'll live with my actions."

He studied her brave face, knowing he would be dead if she had not risked everything. But reasoning with her would not work, nor would being nice.

"Well, Miss Macgregor, you do wear your martyrdom well." He didn't try to hide his sarcasm. It dripped from each word. She flinched, and a jolt of guilt clenched his gut. However, he didn't regret the comment or the coldness of his voice. Truth be told, it bothered him more than he wanted to admit that this woman would rather be an outcast than his wife.

Her eyes narrowed, color rushing to her face. "What are you talking about?"

"Where are you going to go when people stop talking to you? Or maybe they won't ignore you, but they will hurl nasty comments in your direction."

Her face paled with each remark. His assault was calculated, hitting every fear she probably held, but it had to be done. The woman needed to realize what she was going to face. Sebastian saw it as his duty to save her from herself.

"You have somewhere else to go, Miss Macgregor?" He gave her his best sneer. "I know you don't. You know you don't. What will you do when no one will sit next to you in church or men in town begin to think of you in different terms and decide to visit you when they know you are alone?

"We have to do something because your reputation is at stake here. Living in a little village like this, there is no way you can survive this kind of scandal."

"Don't worry. I'll think of something. I always do." Her laughter had died and her tone turned frosty and distant. She walked away and looked out the window.

She'd been so warm when she laughed, and remorse sliced through him anew, knowing he was to blame for her change. He stamped it down, understanding this was for her best interests. "What will you do?"

She chewed on her thumbnail as if contemplating the fate of the world. Well, she was. Her world.

"I don't know. Mr. Pearson wouldn't say a word, but John..." Her voice trailed off as she succumbed to her thoughts.

John was probably formulating his story as he sat in her house. He would relish telling every person in town about what he witnessed. A woman, no matter the age, no matter her station in life, had to hold herself above reproach. It wasn't fair, but it was the way of English society.

He forced the earlier sarcasm from his voice and gently asked, "Can you afford to lose your reputation?"

She sighed, and he had his answer.

"If people find out about what happened..."

"I'll be ostracized. My life as I know it will be over. Everyone in the village will whisper behind my back, if they don't spit in my face." Her anger held him immobile and stunned him with its viciousness. She whirled around. "I'll lose the only thing I have, my home. Happy now, Mr. Lord Ware? I understand exactly what my choice has cost me." Unshed tears glittered in her eyes.

A beat of silence followed her tirade as Sebastian tried to formulate an answer. He understood her anger, but it did not change the situation.

"Miss Macgregor...Colleen...I—"

"Just go back to your estate and your strumpets, and leave me alone! I should have left you in the snow to die."

The last ended on a sob. She covered her mouth, as if ashamed the sound escaped. He looked at her but said nothing. The woman had saved him. If it had not been for her, he would have surely died, and now his presence would very likely cause her to lose her home.

Marriage. He had never thought to marry again. Being second in line for an earldom there was no need. His cousin had married recently and was in good health. Sebastian's marriage had taught him that he was not cut out for a long-term commitment. But...

She turned back to the window, her arms crossed beneath her breasts.

"You want to tell me why you disdain marriage?"

Her voice was wooden when she spoke, the earlier emotion drained. "My parents had a wonderful marriage, but when my father died, my mother was lost. Two years later, she met the drunk. It was horrible, but she was stuck with him. Then there is Deidre."

"Deidre?"

"My sister. She became a mistress for a nobleman who was here for a while. When she became pregnant, she was so sure he would marry her."

"What happened?"

The laugh that escaped reeked of bitterness. He found himself longing for the joy he'd heard earlier, even if it was at his expense.

"It seems he forgot to mention he was married to a woman he left behind in London. There was no way he would leave his wife for a tramp like her. When she threatened to tell his wife, he beat her. She lived long enough to lose the baby." She glanced at him, then looked away and swallowed. "So you see, I've not seen a pretty picture of marriage."

"No, I suppose not." How could he convince this woman to let him do this? He understood her unique position. She had an independent life with no apparent need to marry. She had money to survive, a home, and that meant that she did not need a husband. It would take a miracle to change her mind. As he thought the situation over, an idea formed, one that would work if she were to agree to the deception.

"No one will know we married."

She turned, her eyes narrowed. "Isn't that the idea?"

He glanced at the opened door. "Colleen, why don't you come closer?" She shot him a suspicious look. "I just thought we should discuss this between ourselves, without others being able to hear." He waited for her to draw closer. Lowering his voice, he continued, "I mean no one in London would know. I wasn't planning on marrying again. But no one there would know."

"And?"

"Well, I could leave, make up some story about having to go home, then I can send some sort of message that I died. You'd regain your respectability."

She stared at him as if he had lost his mind. "Really, and once you have me sign the papers and say the vows, what then? You forget to leave, keep my house and expect husbandly rights?"

He chuckled. "No need to worry about that, love."

She frowned harder.

"I have plenty of land to keep me happy and plenty of women to keep me busy."

"Hmm. So, you would sign a contract allowing for me to keep the house?"

"No problem. It will work, Miss Macgregor." He could see her contemplating her fate. She was going to take the bait, he just knew it.

"Well, as long as you sign a contract and swear that you will send the message you've died, I agree."

"How about we seal the bargain with a kiss?"

"In your dreams, Lord Drunk." She studied him for a moment. "Why would you want to marry a woman you hardly know?"

He searched his mind, but he really couldn't come up with a logical conclusion other than the one discussed. "You will lose your reputation if I don't."

She sighed and turned to look out the window again. "There is that."

He wished he could stand, cross the room and take her in his arms. Anything to wipe away the troubles that seemed to weigh so heavily on her mind. His need to comfort and reassure her made him pause. Other than his sister and mother, he had never wanted to soothe the troubles of another female.

"It really leaves us no choice." Her back stiffened when he spoke, and he knew he was pushing her, but he didn't care. He would not allow this woman to self-destruct because of pride.

"I...I really can't understand why you would give up your chance for marriage. You must have the whole English notion of leaving heirs and a fortune to protect your women. Besides, I'm sure you are in the scandal sheets on a regular basis. Everyone will know that you are not dead."

He chuckled at the thought that his mother and younger sister needed him to survive. "Yes, but not by the name you just introduced me. I am Lord Penwyth as per my family title. Not Ware. They'll never know.

"And because I have an uncle with a very healthy, albeit, distant cousin, one who married just last year, I have no title really to leave an heir. My 'women' as you call them would resent that you think they need me."

She paced in front of him. "Why? Why would you do this? You will not lose anything if you jump on a horse tomorrow. So why don't you go?" She stopped in front of him at the end of her question, her grey eyes shining with bewilderment and uncertainty.

After hearing some of her experiences, he realized she had not had many reasons to depend on a man, or even trust him to do the right thing. Until this moment he never thought he would be a man who would aspire to change her misconceptions.

"Listen, Colleen."

She fisted her hands and placed them on her hips. "I did not give you leave to use my first name."

"Well, we are to be married, are we not?" She still glowered at him, but he decided to forge ahead. "You saved my life. I never want to marry again. Elizabeth was a conniving, duplicitous bitch who cared nothing for anyone, even herself. My parents had a wonderful marriage, but they are rare in the ton." He paused, trying to formulate an answer that would help his case for marriage.

"I don't ever want to go through what I went through before. No one will suspect in my social circles, mainly because it is well known I have sworn off marriage. What I do understand is obligation. You saved my life, even when you thought I was a drunk. Let me do this for you. I will marry you, leave for London, and never bother you again."

CRCBCR

Less than a week later, Colleen found herself a married woman—the one thing in the world she thought she would never be. She sat at her dining table staring out at the melting snow, wondering what her mother would think about this turn of events. Knowing her, she would be overwhelmed with joy that a man had finally come to Colleen's rescue.

Mrs. Pearson and Gerty had thrown together a small wedding and reception. It had ended an hour earlier, her husband retiring to pack his things for his trip tomorrow. If anyone thought it strange her husband was leaving the morning after his wedding they didn't mention it. Oh, she was sure Mr. Pearson was chomping at the bit to voice his opinions on the illustrious Mr. Ware, but either he decided to let it go or

Mrs. Pearson had threatened him. More than likely it was the latter.

Most of York was still recovering from the snowstorm that hit Sunday last, but the roads were clear enough for travel. Sebastian had used the excuse of riding back to London to deal with some business matters. Since he had been gone a over a fortnight, he needed to return and tend to things. He explained that he would return soon, but it had been so long, he worried his family would think him lost and begin to panic.

Sebastian had relocated to the inn as soon as the snow had been cleared, but he had moved back to her cottage earlier that day. They had yet to settle the business of her home. She hoped he held to his agreement because she really didn't know what people would think if she coshed her husband on his head on their wedding night.

Her thoughts drifted to her wedding ceremony and the kiss to seal the vows. Sebastian had looked down into her eyes, a trace of apology in his. She had tensed when he bent his head. Her nerves had caused her to lick her lips and she heard a small groan from Sebastian as his gaze followed the movement.

His mouth was undemanding at first. No intrusion, no attack. She had relaxed thinking because of the occasion he would behave. Then, his tongue traced the seam of her lips and without a thought, she willingly opened her mouth to allow him access. It was Sebastian who put a stop to the kiss, pulling back from her with a confident smile.

She could still feel the impression of his lips against hers, and she did not like it at all. Just remembering the kiss lit a fire in her blood. A tingle of something she did not quite understand slipped down her spine. Shifting on her chair, Colleen tried her best to force the memory from her mind.

A soft knock sounded at the door, thankfully breaking into her thoughts of lips, tingles and tongues. Knowing Sebastian had asked John to come by to take him into town, she sighed and slowly stood.

She walked to the door, wondering why her stomach clenched in panic when she thought of Sebastian leaving. It was exactly what she wanted, what she needed. She didn't need some rake flirting with her, kissing her silly, driving her mad with ideas of just what was beyond the kisses he offered.

She opened her front door and found a stately woman dressed in unrelieved black standing on her doorstep. Beside her stood a woman close to Colleen's age, perhaps slightly younger, anxiety in her ice blue eyes.

"Young lady," the older woman said in a perfect aristocratic accent. "I've been told Mr. Sebastian Ware is residing here."

Oh, Lord, was this the Beatrice he spoke of? This woman was old enough to be his mother! Yet, she could understand the attraction. Small boned with blonde hair, and the delicate features of the typical English rose, the woman would draw the eye of most men. Even though she placed the woman's age over fifty, a woman like this would attract men for years to come.

"He is at the moment." She noticed the younger woman relax and shiver. Realizing the wind had turned a bit cooler, she decided she couldn't leave the women standing outside. "Forgive me. Come out of the cold." She hurried the women into her parlor and urged them close to the fire.

"We would appreciate if you would retrieve him for us," the younger woman said. Colleen glanced at the younger woman who was also dressed in black. Both women wore the latest fashions and the finest fabrics. The dark colors suggested they had lost a family member.

Dreading the idea of hosting Sebastian's lover in her home didn't erase years of good training from her mother.

"I would be more than happy to if you would be so kind as to give me your names."

"What the bloody hell are you two doing here?" Sebastian boomed from the entrance to the room. He strode forward and stopped when he reached her side. His fisted hands rested on his lean hips and his eyes narrowed as he looked at the two women.

"Sebastian, is that any way to speak to your mother?"

Chapter Five

Sebastian stared, his mind completely fixed on the idea that he'd had quite a bit of bad luck lately. It apparently wasn't getting much better. When he'd heard his mother's cultured voice as he descended the stairs, he thought he'd been mistaken. There would be no reason for his mother to be in York, in the home of his wife, asking after him. He had worried he was having a relapse.

But there stood his mother, along with his meddling sister who beamed up at him.

"Sebastian," Anna fairly shouted as she ran and jumped into his arms. He picked her up off the ground and then set her back down, giving her a kiss on her cheek. He looked at his mother, and she was dabbing her eyes. "We've been looking for you forever, Sebastian. Mother had to hire someone to find you."

"I am only a few weeks late."

"Yes, but we could not find you," his mother said, her voice wavering. "And there has been...been so much..."

His sister hurried over and comforted their mother. A feeling of dread settled over him. His mother was not a wilting flower of a woman, and for her to behave as such, something horrible must have happened.

Anna looked at him, tears lingering in her eyes. "When Uncle Albert died, then Cousin Gilbert, well, Mother thought the worse."

"Uncle Albert died?" Grief swamped him as his throat closed. His father had died when Sebastian was only seventeen, and Albert had stepped in and guided him through the next few years, making sure the family was settled. He swallowed. "Gilbert?"

Anna stared at him and then glanced behind him. He looked over his shoulder. Colleen had distanced herself from the three of them, moving almost all the way out of the room. She appeared ready to bolt and leave him to his family.

Although he understood her reaction, he did not like it. His wife should be standing by his side. It was an irrational thought, but he couldn't help it.

Good Lord. He'd forgotten he'd married.

"Colleen, please come forward and meet my mother and sister."

She hesitated, just enough to irritate him, but she eventually walked to his side, albeit sullenly. That broom handle stiffened in her back. She glared up at him, and the light glinted off her lenses. Her brow furrowed in a scowl, warning him he would pay for this later.

"Mother. Anna. This is Colleen Macgregor. Colleen Macgregor Ware." His mother's eyes widened as she looked from him to Colleen and then back. For once, his mother held her tongue. "Colleen, may I present my mother, Lady Victoria, and my sister, Lady Anna."

Silence filled the room. Uncomfortable with the study his mother was giving Colleen, he draped his arm over her shoulders, pulling her close to his side. The smell of cinnamon and honey surrounded him, and the heat of her body warmed his. It had him thinking of things he shouldn't.

It reminded him of that kiss. That one little clumsy kiss she gave him at the wedding had him regretting his agreement to not demand his husbandly rights.

Lord knew he'd been kissed by women who had been trained to tease, to entice. It was clear that Colleen had not been kissed often and was completely untutored in the art of seduction. But the moment she opened her mouth and accepted his tongue was one of the most erotic experiences of his life. The memory sent fire racing along his nerve endings. He shifted, trying to ease the tightness of his britches. How this one, too tall, judgmental, red-haired prude did this to him, he didn't know. But she did.

His sister rushed forward once more, breaking his thoughts. "Oh, Sebastian, is it true? Did you really marry?" She hugged him again and then grabbed his wife and hugged her. She released Colleen and clapped. "Oh. Oh, a sister. I have a sister!"

Colleen wore an expression of wary amazement. Sebastian knew the feeling. Everyone, save his best friend Daniel, was usually held speechless when his sister went full force. Anna was far and away one of the most demonstrative people he knew, especially in the constricting environment of society. But he was also thankful. She'd smoothed over an awkward moment.

Colleen cleared her throat, and a fine blush worked up her cheeks. She shot him a dirty look. "Thank you, Lady Anna. Why don't you make yourselves comfortable while I make tea?"

"Oh, that would be wonderful, Colleen. You know, it is so very cold outside, and Mother and I were wandering forever trying to find this place. There is a lot of confusion here because of the blizzard. Do you want some help fetching the tea?"

He almost laughed out loud when Colleen agreed, knowing his sister would drive her batty. Anna linked her arm through Colleen's and winked at Sebastian as she passed him. He watched them leave, and as soon as the door clicked, he knew his mother would not hold back any longer.

"Sebastian, what on earth is going on?"

He turned and looked at his mother. In her late fifties, she was still a very attractive woman. On any other day, there was a sparkle in her blue eyes, and she was always ready with some sort of witty joke. Her sense of humor, along with what they called bluestocking ways, had made her an Original during her first year in the ton. The story was that his father apparently had to fight off several suitors, many of whom started reappearing within a year of his father's death. Although he knew she'd had more than one or two offers of marriage, she'd turned down every one.

She was a good mother, patient and loving, tender but strong. Since reaching majority, he had enjoyed their relationship. At the moment though, memories of being called onto the carpet flitted across his mind. He felt as if he were eight years old again.

"Mother, let's get your wet cloak off of you, and then I'll explain." He helped remove her cloak, then escorted her to a pair of comfortable chairs near the fire. After she was settled, he joined her in the chair opposite. "A week ago, Miss Macgregor found me passed out in the snow, the day the blizzard struck."

She frowned at him, her finely arched eyebrows wrinkled in disapproval. "*Sebastian.* You've never been given to drink."

"Well, I hadn't then, either. I'd been hit on the head. She brought me inside and nursed me back to health." He went on to explain how sick he had been, and just how much Colleen had done to save him. "Unfortunately, the vicar found me with her in her bedroom, and so the marriage was forced."

"She trapped you into marriage?" Outrage filled her voice.

He laughed, and his mother's eyes narrowed. "No, I can assure you she did not. She's none too happy about being married to me."

Immediately her outrage turned another corner. "Why, what is wrong with the girl? I'll have a talk with her and set her straight. She should be overjoyed to have you as her—"

He laughed again, stopping her defense of him. "Thank you, Mother, but that's really not needed. No, really," he said, grabbing his mother's hand as she rose from her chair. She reseated herself and gave him a good frown. "No, listen, the idea was I would send her news of my death when I returned to London. She wouldn't marry me without that one promise. I didn't know what else to do, Mother. If I did not marry her, she would have lost her reputation and probably this house. It is the one thing she has left in the world. That is not the way to pay back a woman who saved my life."

Her eyes softened, a slight smile curving her lips. "You were always such a good lad." She raised her hand to his cheek as she had when he was young. "Always taking in those strays. Drove your father mad when you snuck in that mongrel... What did you name her?"

"Winifred."

She stood and walked to the window. "Winnie. She was a good dog."

"Yes, she was." He remembered sneaking her in, and the staff helping him to hide her for a week. "Father was furious for a whole day."

His mother chuckled. "Yes, yes, he was irritated with you on that one."

"Mother." He waited for her to turn. "What are the two of you doing here?"

"Well, we sent word to you about Albert, but we never heard back. It's been so long since we've seen you."

He had left over six months ago. Usually happy to pursue town interests, Sebastian had an overwhelming surge of restlessness fill his blood during the last year. After a brief stint through continental Europe, he'd traveled to Freddy Crammer's house for a party. Just two days before his mishap, he had made arrangements to return to town. Although not very eager to resume his old life, he had missed his mother and sister.

"I know, Mother. I missed you and Anna. That was why I was coming home last week. Now, what is this about Albert?"

"Your uncle had the accident, then..." She sighed, her cool tone melting in a wave of sadness Sebastian could feel in his soul. "...then, Gilbert. We never expected it to happen to both of them so close together."

"Both of them?" Dread settled in his stomach. "What happened, Mother?"

Tears gathered in her eyes. "They are dead, Sebastian. You are the new Earl of Penwyth."

C3CBCR

"I'm so very excited to have you as a sister."

Colleen sighed as she lifted the tea tray. She knew Anna was excited about having her as a sister. She had told Colleen the same thing at least five times in fifteen minutes. Used to her solitary house with only Gerty with whom to visit, Colleen was not comfortable with someone so talkative.

Sebastian's sister prattled nonstop about the most inane things. From the snow, to being happy she had a sister, to London, she talked, taking nary a breath. It was little wonder why Sebastian was so quiet. There was no way a person could get a word in edgewise with Lady Anna.

"Oh, and we will have so much fun shopping once we reach London. With your red hair and those eyes, you would look wonderful in green. It's been five months since Albert's death, three weeks since Gilbert's, so you should be able to wear the darker shades and not cause a scandal. But," she said, her brow furrowing as she studied Colleen, "I think you would look marvelous in black or something like amethyst."

Anna followed Colleen and continued to blabber about everything they would do in London. Colleen didn't have the heart to tell the young woman she would not be going with them. Although her incessant chatter was driving Colleen insane, there was a warmth about Anna, something totally accepting and loving that caused Colleen to hold her tongue.

After Anna opened the door, Colleen hurried forward, hoping to end this uncomfortable meeting. She knew his mother was not happy he married a no one from the wilds of York any more than Colleen was happy to have them in her drawing room.

Sebastian stood by the window, his mother in his arms as she wept.

"Ah, here's Colleen and Anna with the tea. I'm sure she talked Colleen's ear off."

Colleen set the tea tray on the table.

"That is not nice to say, Sebastian. You haven't seen me in months and now you complain." Anna's voice belied her comments, telling Colleen that the siblings enjoyed a warm relationship. She pushed away the pang of loss and jealousy she felt. Deidre and she had never shared a close relationship, at least not since their adolescence.

"Hush, brat. Even though you just proved my point."

Anna smiled at her brother and wandered to a chair. After she was settled, he moved his attention back to his mother. "Now then, Mother, let's take some tea."

He escorted her to her chair while Colleen poured the tea. She turned to sit on the sofa and bumped into Sebastian. He took her arm, a smile twitching his lips. The heat of his hand warmed her through her sleeve. She shivered. He seated her and then sat beside her. For several moments, they drank tea in silence. It was almost unbearable. She knew his mother wanted to know how she'd trapped him into marriage. Why else would he marry her?

"Mother was telling me we had some unfortunate accidents in the family."

She looked at Sebastian. He'd gained all of his strength back, and she had trouble concentrating when he stared at her. No longer weak, he was the epitome of male beauty. His color had returned, the golden hue reminding her of the moments she had seen him almost naked.

On more than one occasion, his cool blue eyes caused her tongue to tangle and heart to almost jump out of her chest. She tried to turn her attention away to gain her composure but found her gaze traveling to his lips. They were full and sensuous, and all she could remember was the way they tasted when he kissed her. She licked her lips at the memory. His then twitched slightly, and her gaze shot to his. The mocking glint in his eyes told her he knew what she'd been thinking.

Pulling herself from her thoughts, she asked, "Really, wh-what kind of accidents?"

Sebastian's smile faded. She found herself regretting her question.

"Well, it seems that my uncle and cousin died recently."

"Oh," she said and looked at his mother and sister. "I'm so sorry for your loss."

Sebastian stared down at her, irritated at the relief he heard in her voice. His continued presence worried her more than his dead relatives. Didn't she even care that he was leaving? He was her husband for Christ's sake.

Because of his irritation, his voice was a tad rougher when he spoke. "Yes, I have to take over the estate."

"The estate?" Her voice rose as she asked the question. Both his mother and sister stared at her, then at him.

"Yes, dear, Sebastian must take up the reigns of the earldom." His mother offered this.

Colleen's eyes widened then narrowed when she looked at him.

"Earldom?" Her voice was hoarse.

"Yes, *darling*, you are the new Countess of Penwyth."

Color seeped from her face, leaving her pale, and he felt a twinge of guilt. He wasn't all that happy about the situation, but he would be damned if he allowed her to push him out now.

The need to gain her acceptance of their marriage rode high in his priorities. He knew it had more to do with personal feelings than their uncomfortable position. Just that thought alone was enough to make him uncomfortable. It wasn't a dream come true for him, but he would appreciate it if the woman didn't act as if she were being condemned to death.

Sebastian sat back with his arms crossed and enjoyed the show. This was one of the few times he had seen her at a loss for words.

"Isn't it exciting?" Anna said. Her bubbly voice made Colleen twitch.

He smothered a laugh. The woman was going to give him hell as soon as they were alone. He looked forward to the battle. Sparring with Colleen was more exciting than any seduction he'd encountered. If she raised her voice to him, he might just have to kiss her. That thought sent warmth speeding through him, heating his blood. He shifted his weight, trying to relieve some of the tension his musings brought.

"Exciting?" Colleen asked, her voice rising an octave.

"Oh, yes." Anna was oblivious to her sister-in-law's distress. "Here I thought we would have to put up with all those insipid girls trying to catch themselves an earl, but now we have you. And you are ever so pleasant. Isn't she, Sebastian?"

He thought of that wedding kiss, the feel of her lips against his, the way she had tasted... "Why, yes, she is." His voice had taken on a husky edge as his gaze slipped to her lips.

"Really, Sebastian," his mother admonished.

Her voice brought him out of all thoughts of kissing, tasting. When he looked at her, he could tell from the expression on her face she knew what he was thinking. His face flushed in embarrassment.

"Now, we will have to leave as soon as possible. You are going to be presented to society, and I'm sure we'll have a lot of shopping to do."

Colleen said not a word as she listened to his mother. If he didn't know better, he'd have thought she was not a bit upset. Then he saw she was clenching her teacup so tightly, it was a wonder it didn't shatter.

"Listen, Mother, Colleen and I need to talk about this. Why don't you and Anna go back to the inn, rest and then we'll have dinner?"

His mother looked from him to Colleen and then back again to him. A shrewd expression entered her eyes.

"Yes. That sounds like a marvelous idea."

രുജ്ഞരു

As the carriage pulled away, Victoria Ware settled against the seat.

Anna's bubbly voice broke the silence. "I had no idea he would ever marry again."

Victoria looked at her daughter, nineteen and so full of dreams and warmth. "He vowed not to. But...I think he got more than he bargained for with this one."

"What do you mean, Mother?"

She grimaced, thinking of the way that tramp of a first wife had hurt her son. She'd not wanted him to marry so young, but he said he was in love so she had agreed. It had proved to be the wrong decision. Not six months later, she had started cheating on Sebastian and was dead a year after that from a jealous lover's bullet.

"Yes, well, they married under unusual circumstances." Victoria stopped Anna when she opened her mouth to ask questions. "You do not need to know anything about it. It is private and between them."

Anna pouted for a minute and then smiled. "Well, the way he looks at her..." She sighed.

Oh, yes. She'd seen the way her son studied his wife. Sebastian was no choirboy. She knew he'd had many women.

But when he looked at Colleen, it reminded her of her own dear Edward.

She thought about her plain daughter-in-law. There was something so familiar about those eyes. That shade of grey danced at the edge of a memory. She shook her head, knowing her mind was still not working properly. The last few weeks had been trying, worrisome and downright horrible. With the stress the family had already endured, tension had ridden high when Sebastian did not return on time.

One thing was for certain. She would do everything in her power to make sure there was no annulment. As she closed her eyes, she remembered the look on her son's face while he watched Colleen, and the daggers her daughter-in-law had shot at him with her gaze.

She smiled. Oh, yes indeed. Those two would give her wonderful grandchildren.

CRCБCR

Colleen sat on her bed, anger boiling her blood. She could not believe what a mess they had made of things. What were they going to do now? She had to find some way to break out of this ridiculous muddle. She didn't want a husband. Now she was stuck with one *and* a bloody title.

Sebastian entered the bedroom and shut the door behind him. He leaned against it, crossing his arms. He didn't say anything for a few moments, but he studied her, his gaze moving from her head down to her toes and back up again.

"Well, let's hear it."

"Let's hear it?" She couldn't believe he was being so casual. "Let's hear it?"

"I know you are dying to yell at me, so let it go." He gestured with his hands casually, as if he were asking for the price of a cravat.

"Yell at you?" Her voice was a hoarse whisper as she tried to contain her anger.

"Really, Colleen, you are beginning to sound like a simpleton. You keep repeating everything I'm saying. You did the same thing with my mother and sister. It's a wonder they don't think you have some kind of mental deficiency."

The gall of the man! He was accusing her of acting like an idiot. And there he stood, behaving as though there was nothing wrong. For the first time in her adult life, rage took over.

Glancing around, trying to calm her heart—which was beating so fast she was amazed she didn't expire on the spot—she noticed her favorite brush lying on her bed. She grabbed it and flung it at him with all her might. He ducked, and the brush banged against the door before falling to the floor.

"What the bloody hell are you doing?"

"I'm acting like a simpleton!"

He smiled. It warmed his eyes and softened his features. A whisper of misgiving brushed over her skin. The man was deadly when he turned on the charm. "I was only joking with you. Trying to ease the tension."

"Sebastian! You said we would not get caught. Now we are trapped and not only that, your mother and sister think I am going to London with you."

He looked away from her and walked to the window. "Would it be that bad, Colleen? You've never been there. You could see all the sights."

"And then what? Wait until the annulment is fulfilled?"

He didn't say anything. The clock ticked, the only sound in the room. The silence lingered and the tension tightened. Her suspicions rose and almost choked her.

"We *are* getting an annulment."

"Colleen, that might be a problem."

She didn't say anything. She couldn't. Her mind now whirled with the implications of what that simple statement meant.

He turned, an apologetic smile on his face. "I'm an earl, Colleen. It makes for a sticky situation."

Sebastian tried to keep his thoughts on their conversation but it was proving difficult. Colleen's face flushed with anger again. God, she was a sight to be seen when she was annoyed. A few strands had escaped her pulled-back hair and curled under her chin. His fingers itched to tuck them behind her ear. Or, thread his fingers through the heavy mass, causing it to fall.

With each angry breath, her chest rose and fell, drawing his attention to her breasts. The bodice of her dress left little to be desired, but in her anger, the soft, worn fabric hugged against her breasts, clinging to the curves with each inhalation.

Momentarily, he thought of stripping away the fabric, revealing just what she looked like naked. Ideas of gliding his hands over her skin tumbled through his mind. He could just imagine teasing, arousing, drawing her passion from her as he delighted in taking his own pleasure. Suddenly, painfully, he needed to know what her breasts looked like.

Were they pale with rose-tipped nipples that would tighten the moment he brushed his fingers over them?

"A sticky situation?"

Her voice brought him back to the present, although he had to shift again, to try to ease the heaviness of his groin.

"Yes. An annulment will be hard to obtain."

"What does that mean?"

"It means that we may have to stay married."

Slowly she rose and walked to him, her hands on her hips. "You said there would be no problem. No one would know we were married."

She was close enough for her sweet scent to reach him, surround him. Jesus, it made him want to nibble her neck and work his way down to more interesting parts.

"Well, there is a slight problem with that. My mother knows."

"You said you told her the truth."

She had the most magnificent pair of lips. They were plump, the bottom one a little fuller than the top. Her untutored kisses almost made him lose control. With a little practice and some help from him, she would be exquisite. Thoughts of teaching her, kiss by kiss, sent another rush of heated blood through his veins.

"Sebastian! Are you paying attention to me?"

"Yes. I am." He cleared his throat and pulled his mind from teaching his wife to kiss. "Mother would never lie about me being married."

There had come a point in his discussion with his mother that he had realized they would have to stay married. He was obligated to produce an heir. She had risked her reputation to save his life. While physically she wasn't his usual type of woman, she had a quick wit and sinful lips.

And she smelled of hot rolls.

"What are you saying?" Her voice was just above a whisper. He smiled, trying to reassure her.

"I'm saying that maybe we should reconsider our arrangement."

Chapter Six

All color drained from Colleen's face. Sebastian grabbed her arm to be sure she didn't pass out. From the look on her face, one would think being married to him was a fate worse than death. Not that he thought himself to be the catch of the season, but it was damned irritating that the thought of marriage almost sent his wife into a dead faint.

"Reconsider our arrangement?" she asked hoarsely. "What makes you think...?" She jerked her arm out of his hand. "What makes you think I want to continue this *arrangement*?"

"Good Lord, woman, sit down before you faint."

The reprimand was enough to bring her back to life. Her face flushed, and her nostrils flared. That handle tightened in her back. Thank God she had her pride and tenacity. He could never deal with fainthearted women.

"I do not have fainting spells. I'm sure the women you acquaint yourself with—"

"What an interesting term, 'acquaint'. I've never thought about it that way."

Her eyes rounded, and she sputtered. Actually sputtered! Deciding he had the upper hand, he changed the subject.

"We are in a bit of a predicament, you and I."

"You signed a contract. You said you would send a telegram of your death."

He shook his head. "Colleen, that would never hold up, and what are you going to do? Take me to the justices? Let the whole world know that we struck a bargain?"

"Everyone in this town knows I despise titled men."

"We live in a society that would never side with you in court."

Her shoulders slumped and her lip quivered. "You said you would stick to the bargain and leave me alone." Her voice was flat, emotionless. He did not like it at all. He liked her breathing fire and spitting insults.

"That was before Mother showed up. She'd throw a fit if I denied her wishes. It isn't as if I'm thrilled about this arrangement either, Colleen. I never planned on marrying again."

She walked around the bed and paced in front of her door. The dress she wore was a horrible shade of brown, buttoned up to her throat. It sagged in the bodice and the design made her look like a giraffe. Still, he couldn't help watching the sway of her hips as she marched back and forth.

"There has to be a way out of this!"

"There is, but it would ruin your reputation." He leaned against the windowsill, crossing his arms. "I know that it isn't fair, but I'd not be touched by the scandal. Oh, I'm sure there would be a few invitations I would miss, but well, I'm an earl."

Even as the words left his mouth, he couldn't fathom his new position. He'd never thought to be an earl, happy to be the only son of a second son. All the money, none of the work. Taking the reigns of the estate would not be difficult, but to be the result of such a tragedy left a hollow pit in his stomach.

"If anything, it would make me all the more interesting, especially to women."

That comment brought her pacing to a stop. She turned on him, slowly stomping in his direction. "You mean to say…" She took a deep breath as if trying to calm her nerves. "You would use my downfall as a way to acquire more women?" Her voice cracked on the last word.

"Ah, you care. I can't tell you what that means to me."

Her eyes narrowed and then turned steel grey. She continued closer and stopped within inches of him. Once again, the scent of hot sticky buns surrounded him and he found himself fighting not to lick his lips.

"If we are going to make this marriage permanent, which seems to be the case, I think you need to become more accommodating," he said.

There! Acting like she was above being married to him. He was so busy being pleased with himself, he never saw the punch coming.

Colleen screamed in pain when her fist connected with his nose. The crunch of bone filled the room, and she wasn't sure if it was her hand or his nose. He cursed, his hands flying to his face.

Tears gathered in her eyes as pain radiated from her knuckles up her arm. Her fingers tingled then went numb. She grabbed her fingers and collapsed on the bed.

"Why are you crying, Colleen? You broke my nose!" His voice was pinched and muffled. He was holding one of his monogrammed handkerchiefs up to his nose, blood quickly soaking the fine linen and oozing over his hands.

She'd broken the man's nose. Colleen Marie Macgregor lost her temper and broke a man's nose. Her head was spinning from her momentary surge of anger and complete wonder. She flexed her fingers and winced at the pain, but she was happy she could move them. "I hurt my hand on your hard nose."

"Serves you right."

"Good Lord, you are a baby. So I broke your nose."

With cool blue eyes, he looked down at her. "Well, this does not bode well for our marriage, Mrs. Ware."

"Yes, you better make sure you carry on the tradition of English nobility, my lord earl, and sleep in a separate room. Just be certain to lock the door in between them."

He stared at her, his eyes widening as her words sank in. "Are you threatening me?"

"I'm promising you that if you even think of holding me to this ridiculous marriage, you will fear for your life. Every night you will wonder if I will sneak into your room and stab you with a knife."

"I promise you, Colleen"—his voice was soft as a kitten's purr but lethal to her composure as it skated down her spine— "if you sneak into my room at night, I'll be able to interest you in more entertaining nocturnal activities."

CRCBCR

Dinner was a strained affair. Both of Sebastian's eyes were blackened, his nose swollen, so it was decided they would dine in Colleen's home. Sebastian sat at the head of the table, scowling and sniping at her at every turn. He had no reason to be so hateful.

She looked at his swollen nose. Deciding he might have a tiny reason—okay a pretty big reason—to be irritated with her, she tried her best to be pleasant. To tell the truth, she was ashamed of what she had done. Her parents had always taught her not to strike another living thing in anger. Never in all her days had anyone, man or beast, caused her blood to boil the way Sebastian did.

"Oh, Colleen, you set such a pretty table." Lady Anna sat on her right, a genuine smile on her face, her blue eyes sparkling.

She couldn't help but return the smile. "Thank you, Anna. I do love to cook."

Sebastian mumbled something she could not hear, then snorted. His mother shot him a hard look, and he quieted.

"Oh, Miss Macgregor, er...Ware... Oh, sweet heavens, what do we call you?" Mrs. Pearson asked.

"Mrs. Ware is fine with me."

"Lady Penwyth," Sebastian said, but this time he ignored his mother's look. His voice was hard and his gaze never wavered. "You are to be called Lady Penwyth."

She tightened her jaw as she felt her temper rising yet again. It didn't take much where Sebastian was involved. "But I am fine with Mrs. Ware."

His blue eyes darkened, his lips flattened. "You are a countess, and you will be called according to your title."

"Really, Sebastian, don't take that tone with me."

The vicar, his wife and Colleen's in-laws watched in fascination, their heads swinging from one end of the table to the other.

"I will take any kind of tone..." He stopped, apparently realizing they were squabbling like a couple of children.

Silence descended on the room. Nothing but the sound of silverware against her mother's best china filled the air.

"Well, it is still hard to believe that you were just an orphan, no relations to hear of, and now, you are a countess," said Mrs. Pearson, her kind voice releasing some of the gathered tension.

"You really have no family?" asked Anna.

"No. My father died when I was twelve, my mother a few years ago. My sister died last year. I do have some family in south England on my mother's side and Scotland on my father's side."

"Why did you not go to them when you found yourself alone?" This came from her mother-in-law.

"Why would I? Really, I'm self-sufficient. My mother...well, she wasn't the strongest of women, and my sister took after her. I tended the bills and the house from an early age. Besides, my parents married against their families' wishes."

Victoria's eyes twinkled as she studied Colleen. "Do you happen to know your mother's maiden name?"

"No. I think she never really overcame her family's lack of support."

"Lack of support?" Sebastian inquired.

Oh, so now he decided not to pout anymore? She turned in his direction and inwardly cringed at the injuries she'd given him. She didn't know if it was her imagination or not but they seemed to be getting worse.

"My mother married my father, a second son with no money, and worse than that, a Scot. I understand they spirited away to Gretna Green."

He studied her for a moment then asked, his voice ripe with condemnation, "And she felt she could not forgive them for not accepting such idiotic behavior?"

"Idiotic behavior?" Her voice had turned shrill, surprising her and the Pearsons. Colleen Macgregor did not speak in the tone of a fishwife.

"Yes, what would you call it?" When she didn't answer him, he continued. "Their families didn't agree with their marriage, and they ran off. Not very smart."

She clutched her fork so tightly her knuckles were white. What would he do if she stabbed him in the leg with a fork? She hated violence of any kind, but with Sebastian around, she couldn't help it. He seemed to bring it out in her. Not a good sign if their marriage did become permanent.

"But, Sebastian, that's what you did, is it not?" Anna said. "Well, not the running away and marrying against your family's wishes, but you married so fast I'm sure it was because you couldn't wait."

Someone snorted, and she was sure it was Mrs. Pearson. She watched Sebastian's sneer smooth and turn into a mask of a smile. When he spoke, his snide tone had melted into the perfectly pitched intonation of a gentleman.

"Of course you are right, puss." When he glanced at his sister, his eyes warmed, and Colleen's heart skipped a beat. Lord, he was handsome even with his swollen nose and black eyes.

"Well, although I would enjoy nothing more than to take some more time to get to know you better, we need to start making plans for our return," Victoria said. Colleen smiled at her mother-in-law. Even under the unusual circumstances, she'd accepted Colleen. "We will get up bright and early tomorrow and start the plans. I want to leave by Saturday."

"Saturday?" Colleen squeaked. Silently, she counted the days. Panic slid through her. "Three days to get ready. I've too much to do. I need to pack and the house... What am I going to do with the house?"

Although he was still angry with Colleen, Sebastian couldn't help but feel a little sorry for the impertinent woman.

83

Her whole life was about to change, and for this woman, he knew that would be hard. He assumed she was a woman who would not acclimate well to change. She'd cocooned herself in York, hiding from society. If her mother had lived, he doubted Colleen would have turned out differently. She would have easily accepted a bland existence.

"Now, don't you worry," said Mrs. Pearson. "Lord Sebastian and I have had a long discussion on the matter, and I will take over the care of the house. In fact, you could probably find a family willing to rent it." She patted Colleen's hand but his wife didn't appear to notice the gesture.

"But...but this is all I have left." Her eyes shimmered with tears, and Sebastian, knowing his way around her now, decided he'd had enough. She would blame him if she embarrassed herself by breaking down in tears. He would rather she be mad at him.

"We don't have time to lament the loss of your command over your house, Colleen. We need to make plans. Now quit your whining."

His sister and Mrs. Pearson gasped. "Sebastian, really," his mother admonished.

But he paid no heed. He watched Colleen's eyes narrow and darken. That was more like it. She stood and threw her napkin on the table.

"I'll just see to the dishes—"

"No need to worry about that. I will take care of that for you," said Mrs. Pearson as she rose and joined Colleen in clearing the table. "You've had a trying day."

Colleen shot a look at Sebastian that would have stopped his heart dead if she'd had the power. He crossed his arms and returned the look. He was the one with the throbbing nose and black eyes. If Daniel, the Earl of Bridgerton and his best friend, had been present, he'd never hear the end of it. The thought of telling Daniel of his situation, his marriage and the twit he was married to—who would rather waste her life as a spinster—made him cringe.

He turned his attention to his wife, his countess. Too tall, plain and given to horrible fashion choices, she and he were stuck. They went together as well as most couples in society. At least they still spoke at this point, although it had been less than a day. He'd never planned to remarry, but he guessed she was as good as any other.

Her glasses and freckles were not the most attractive but there was a quality, a type of reserved passion he knew he would uncover. She'd been restraining herself for so long she didn't know how to express it. It was the reason he was sitting there with a broken nose.

"Yes, Colleen. You'll need to prepare yourself for our wedding night."

CRCƷCR

Colleen stomped down the hallway and started up the stairs when her mother-in-law stopped her.

"Colleen," she said, waiting for her to turn. "I know you do not know me well, but I would be more than happy to answer any questions you may have."

She cocked her head to one side and studied Lady Victoria. Her smooth ivory skin was pink with embarrassment, and Colleen could not help but smile.

"No, Lady Victoria. You and I know this is no love match, and I see no reason to pretend. Your son has no interest in me, and as soon as his senses clear, he'll realize he really doesn't like me and will grant me an annulment."

"You truly think my son has no interest in you?" Her voice held a tone of pure amazement.

"I know." She stepped forward and impulsively grabbed her mother-in-law's hand. An emotion she could not name choked her as Victoria squeezed her hand around Colleen's. "Your son, from what I gather, likes his women a little different than I. I know I am too tall and gangly and with all this red hair... Well, most men don't like it."

When her mother-in-law looked to protest, Colleen forged ahead. "I've known most of my life how people view me. I have no problem with the fact people do not find me beautiful. I like myself, and that's all that matters."

"You really think yourself plain?"

She chuckled. "I know so. I lived with a mother who was considered a beauty, and a sister who was almost a mirror image of her. I, well, I'm the likeness of my father, except for the eyes. Tall and sturdy, a true Scot."

"Well, I...I know that if Sebastian proves you wrong, well, he will be gentle. He is really a decent man."

"Of course he is. He would never have married me if he weren't."

She didn't know how it happened, but she found herself pulled into Victoria's arms in a crushing embrace. The scent of lavender surrounded her, comforted her. It had been so long since she'd been hugged like this, completely engulfed by a mother's love. Colleen wrapped her arms around her mother-in-law and squeezed with all her might. Tears pricked her eyes when she felt a gentle kiss on her temple.

"You see what other people don't, my dear. Keep that in mind when you deal with Sebastian."

CRCBCR

Sebastian awaited his mother in the parlor, wondering what kind of punishment she would dole out on his head. He'd seen her look when he had teased Colleen, and he knew he was in for a head bashing.

"You're in trouble, you know," his sister said. She sat on one of the sofas, her legs stretched out in front of her.

"Mind your own business, brat. Besides, what the devil is Daniel about letting you two travel on your own? I left you in his care."

One eyebrow rose. The resemblance between his mother and Anna grew every day. She had that imperious, queen-of-the-castle look down pat. "Well, first of all, I don't want you losing this wife. I like her, probably more than I do you. Second of all, we do not need permission from Daniel to do what we please. Mother and I have gotten along just fine without his interference."

"Oh, and what did he say about this little jaunt into the wilds of York?"

"He didn't say anything because he is not my husband," their mother said from the doorway. "Anna, really, sit up. You look like a common tavern wench sitting like that."

"Oh, and when was the last time you saw a tavern wench, Mother?" he asked.

"It's been a while since I've met one of your women, Sebastian." She smiled sweetly. "Don't try to outdo your mother, dear."

"Of course, Mother."

"Anna, please go ready our things. The hour grows late, and I'm ready to retire to the inn."

Anna pouted but did as her mother bid, closing the door on the way out.

"Daniel is probably not happy with us. He'd wanted us to stay in London, but I was irritated with his lack of concern on your part. Your uncle dying was bad enough, but the way your cousin died. I guess our messages kept missing you the way you kept moving around." She shook her head and closed her eyes. He saw the circles bruising the skin beneath her eyes and realized just how troubled she was. For the first time since his father's death, his mother looked fragile.

"I'm sorry, Mother." And he was. He never imagined something like this would happen. The strain on his mother had been great, and even though he hadn't known about the problems, he felt a little guilt for worrying her.

"Yes, well, Daniel said your sister and I were two out-of-control ninny heads with all our thoughts of conspiracy and murder. Your sister and he had a tremendous fight before we left."

"They always fight."

"Not like this one. I fear those two will never talk again." She walked closer and took his hand in hers. "Now, you be kind to your Colleen. She seems strong but there's an underlying vulnerability to her."

"Yes, Mother."

She smiled, and her eyes sparkled.

"I promise."

"That is all I ask of you."

Anna returned with their coats, and the coach awaited them outside. After he bade them good night, he locked the door and walked to the bedroom. It was time to join his wife.

CRCBCR

Colleen, dressed in her favorite white linen nightgown, paced in front of her bed. Irritation and panic had been riding high for the past several minutes. She had no idea just what Sebastian had planned for tonight. Not knowing his intentions, she worried he actually thought to consummate the marriage.

Glimpsing a view of herself in the mirror, she stopped and studied her features. She believed every word she had told her mother-in-law. A little tall, with freckles and a plain face and all of her red hair, she'd known from an early age she was not a beauty. Too many people had told her so. With an older sister whose quiet nature and inward beauty matched her physical appearance, Colleen had lived most of her childhood being compared to her and falling short.

Oh, her parents never compared them, but neighbors, acquaintances, and then as they aged, men did. More than once they were asked if the two of them were really blood related.

Her thick braid fell over her shoulder, a few rebellious strands escaping. She sighed. She wished she had experience dealing with men, but she was sure experience with most of the men in her neighborhood would never have prepared her for her husband.

Her husband.

For a woman who never planned to marry, she found herself in quite a situation. Butterflies filled her stomach. Not only married but married to a rake, and an earl at that.

Footsteps interrupted her thoughts. She jumped into bed and pulled the covers to her chin just as the door was opening.

The breath caught in her throat as he stepped into the room, closing the door behind him. A wolfish smile curved his lips, and she shivered, but not from the cold. And not from fear. His gaze was warm, his eyes cobalt. Heat spread through her, settling in her tummy.

"Well, my Lady, I'm here to claim my husbandly rights."

Chapter Seven

Sebastian inwardly laughed at the expression on his wife's face. Colleen looked much like a goldfish searching for food. Her mouth opened and closed three times as he approached the bed.

He was not such a beast he would require consummation of the marriage this night. At first, the thought of bedding the chit had not really been of any interest to him. But now, the thought of pulling off her prim nightgown and burying himself deep within her had various parts of him standing at attention. He wanted to find out if she smelled of cinnamon everywhere.

Sighing, he knew he could not venture on the hunt for the answer. The day had been stressful, for both of them, but especially for her.

"You...you do not plan..." Her voice trailed off as she closed her eyes. Swallowing, she gathered her courage to ask the question. "You do not plan to force yourself on me, do you?"

"It would not be force, my dear lady. It would be my right to take you, but I would not need to force you."

She opened her eyes and snorted. "I'm not one of your loose women."

"Really? So what you are saying is that to want a man, like a man wants a woman, you have to be a hussy?"

"Yes." She pushed her glasses back up her nose and tilted her chin. "Why would a woman want a man to touch her in such a way?"

He approached the bed. Her eyes widened further with each measured step. His body reacted to her nearness, to the thought of slipping beneath the covers and taking his fill of her. Her pulse fluttered in her neck, a telling sign. The problem was he didn't know if it raced due to fear or arousal.

"Ah, Colleen, a woman, if she were smart, would enjoy her lover's touch."

"Her lover?" She clutched at the covers. "Not her husband?"

"Well, if she were lucky, one and the same."

He had a plan to prove she was a woman of obvious desires. A little design to pay her back for the punch this afternoon. She hid her passions behind those glasses and her attitude, but they were there.

As he sat on the bed, she scooted over so far he was amazed she hadn't fallen on the floor. He suppressed the urge to smile. Colleen would think he was laughing at her, and he didn't want to hurt her feelings. If he did that, his plan would never work.

He removed his shoes and began on his clothes. She yelped when his hands went to his shirt.

"I really must insist you blow out the candles."

Her voice was slightly muffled. He turned and found a mound of covers he presumed to be his wife. She'd hidden for fear of seeing his naked flesh.

Without warning, a memory flashed across his mind. Her lips pressed to his, his tongue in her mouth, the taste of cinnamon and sugar coursing through him. He shook his head to rid himself of the fabrication, but a shimmer of it remained.

He paused in undressing himself and eyed his wifely mound of bedclothes. "Everyone is going to expect me to spend the night here."

"It's just the two of us. No one will know. Many of the aristocracy have separate rooms."

"Not on their wedding night."

"Well, they think we've already had a wedding night."

He couldn't think of a reply to that. He pulled his shirt free of his trousers and tossed it onto the rocking chair situated next to the bed.

"They are not sure. And truthfully, don't you think they would think it odd that I wouldn't want to spend the night with my wife? The wife I married because she nursed me back to health, and I couldn't help but fall in love with her?"

Her snort had him smiling.

"What I don't understand is how you were going to keep it a secret."

He studied her mounded figure still covered by bedclothes. Maybe he should tell her that her lowly station afforded him a certain freedom. He could marry her and leave. They'd never told anyone his title. They knew him as Sebastian Ware, but the truth was nobody called him Lord Ware, using Lord Penwyth instead, his official title. He could return to London and disappear from her life. Easy as that.

"That hardly matters now, does it?" She didn't reply to that. "What were you planning on doing?"

Her comment was muffled.

"What was that?"

She threw the covers aside and sat up. Even in the waning candlelight, he could see her flushed skin and the strands of hair that had escaped her braid. She straightened her glasses.

"I planned on mourning."

"Mourning?"

"Yes." She crossed her arms beneath her breasts. It pulled the fabric tight across them. She was generously endowed, but from what he had witnessed, they were the perfect size for his hands. If he concentrated, he could see the outline of her nipples. "I planned to tell everyone you died."

Heat surged through him. He wanted to see her nipples, free of fabric, basked only in candlelight. His body reacted, his cock hardening at the thought of gliding his fingers over her skin, followed by his tongue. It took a moment for her comment to register.

"Died?" He shoved all thoughts of breasts and nipples and silky skin aside. Well, not all the way to the side, but enough for him to think clearly. He knew this had been their plan all along, but for some reason it was irritating him. Probably because her voice sounded more hopeful about his death than their marriage. "You were going to tell everyone I died? How was I to die?"

She relaxed her arms and played with the quilt. "I...I'm not really sure. I thought something would come to me."

"Something would come to you?" He stared down at the impossible woman. Women in London would kill their own mama to be in her position, and she was plotting his death.

"Sebastian, we both agreed I would tell everyone you died. Remember?"

At the sound of his name on her lips, lust surged. Wisps of her impossible hair tangled around her face, and her glasses slid down her nose. She grazed her bottom lip with her teeth. He almost groaned.

"Say that again."

"We both agreed—"

"No. My name."

Her grey eyes met his and her lips parted.

"Sebastian."

Desire clawed at his belly. His body shook with the need for release.

"Are you feeling all right?" she asked.

"What?"

"You look unwell and your voice sounds funny. I hope you are not having a relapse."

"Relapse?"

She swung her legs to the side of the bed. She stood and rushed to his side. A wave of vanilla surrounded him, enticing him to take a bite. Or a lick. Taking him by the elbow like he was some doddering old simpleton, she led him to the bed.

"Would you like some tea?"

"No."

"You lie down. I'll just settle over there." She motioned to the rocking chair where his shirt now lay.

An idea formed in his mind. If he could appeal to her senses...

"No, you come to bed also."

She hesitated.

"I wouldn't feel right taking over your bed. Please, I promise not to force myself on you tonight."

She studied him a moment longer but relented, walking to the other side. She sat, placed her glasses on the bedside table, extinguished the candle then reclined on the very edge of her side of the bed. Silly woman. She didn't stand a chance.

He cushioned his head on his hands and thought about this woman who was now his wife. Plain, yes and with principles set so high no one could measure up to her ideals. She dressed like a spinster and kissed like a courtesan. He knew she didn't want to face the truth, but there would be no annulment. Even she would understand marriage was the only option. Annulment would make a scandal for him, but it would devastate her standing in her small village. And the news would make it here, especially now that he was an earl.

Her even breathing and relaxed posture told him she had fallen asleep finally. He gently pulled her onto her back. For a moment, he studied her sleeping face. In sleep, she looked innocent. Her skin was translucent. For the first time, he noticed the dark smudges beneath her eyes. She'd been through a tremendous upheaval this week. Prior to that, she'd nursed him back to health.

Peace settled over him. There should be no reason why they could not make a go of this marriage. True, it wasn't a love match. He didn't believe in the silly emotion anyway. But he'd proved tonight he desired her, at least to himself, and she was levelheaded for the most part. Once they were settled in London, he'd explain what needed to be done. She was a good girl with a mind of her own, but she would understand.

She rolled onto her side and cuddled against his bare chest. Her sweet breath warmed his neck as she molded her body to his. Instantly, his member hardened.

Yes, she would agree eventually. He would convince her. As he wrapped his arms around her, he smiled, thinking of all the ways he could convince her and just how much pleasure both of them would gain from his plans.

CRCICR

Six days later, they arrived in London, travel worn and much worse the wear. His Amazon bride did not travel particularly well in a coach. Within ten minutes of stepping foot in the carriage, she became violently ill. And the trip didn't improve. Each night, he'd carried her to her room, placed her on her bed and left her to the ministrations of Betty, his sister's maid. Never in his life would he have suspected strong, hard-willed Colleen would turn into an invalid.

He lifted Colleen down from the carriage and experienced the same heady rush. Blood flowed through him like hot molten lava. He just didn't understand it. Never in his life, even while courting the beautiful Elizabeth, had he felt this surge of awareness of a woman. And for it to happen with this woman— a plain, sharp-tongued spinster—still shocked him.

He stepped down from the carriage and up the steps of his uncle's London residence. Now his by chance. A wave of nostalgia and pain lanced through him. He would never hear his uncle laugh again—never go hunting with his cousin. He swallowed the lump that had formed in his throat. He had busied himself with caring for Colleen the past few days and avoided the pain. And he would continue. He had a mess of an estate and a grieving aunt to tend to. And, he thought, as he shifted Colleen's slight weight, a new wife.

Fitzgerald, the butler of the Penwyth estate for as long as anyone could remember, stood by the massive doors that led into the mansion. Tall, though not as tall as Sebastian, with a wealth of grey hair and bright green eyes, he'd worked for the Penwyth estate his entire life, following in his father's footsteps, and his father before him.

"Fitzgerald, good to see you."

"As well as you, sir." He looked at Colleen, speculation and disapproval dripping from him. Fitzgerald had very high standards.

"I would introduce you to the new countess, but she's not much of a traveler."

Colleen mumbled and shifted in his arms to look up at him. Her clear grey eyes went from confusion to irritation to embarrassment within a moment. Then, in resignation, she closed them.

"Where are we?" Her voice was so quiet he wasn't sure anyone else heard her but him.

"We are home, Colleen." He stepped over the threshold, relishing the warmth of recognition that rushed through him. It had always been the same when he came to visit. There had never been any animosity between his father and his uncle. Close in age and temperament, they tended to gravitate toward each other in family gatherings, sometimes excluding their youngest brother, James.

She groaned and snuggled more closely against him. Well, that was one thing. She trusted him when she was sleeping and ill. Not a fantastic basis for a marriage, but it was a start.

The servants lined the marbled hallway, all waiting to greet their new earl and his wife. Once Colleen felt better, she would blame this embarrassment on him, he was sure of it. For now, he reveled in having her close to him, dependent on him.

His aunt Millicent stood at the base of the grand staircase. A small woman, much like his mother, she resembled what Sebastian thought of as the perfect English rose. Fair skin, fine bone structure, Cupid's bow lips. Unfortunately, the blue eyes that had so often been filled with love and merriment emanated deep, unrelenting pain. Although she stood with the same dignity she had always exuded, an air of defeat surrounded her.

For good reason, losing a husband and son in less than six months.

"Sebastian, Victoria, Anna." She slowly walked forward. The grief in her voice was so profound it nearly unmanned him. Her eyes, which were brimming with tears, shifted to his wife. "I received your message last night."

"Millicent." His mother rushed forward and embraced his aunt. She released Millicent but kept her arm around her waist.

"So much has happened in the last few days. Why don't we go into the parlor while Sebastian takes Colleen upstairs for some much-needed rest?" his mother asked.

Fitzgerald stepped forward. "Refreshments should be ready in a moment. Your rooms are ready if you will follow me, my lord."

Sebastian followed Fitzgerald up the stairs, realizing that for the first time the estate, these servants, his family were all his responsibility.

CR CB CR

"She's Scottish?" asked Prudence, Victoria's younger sister-in-law.

Victoria had never really liked Prudence. A couple years younger, she remembered the woman when she made her debut. A more mean and spiteful debutante had probably never graced the halls of Almack's before or since. She'd been after a duke and then settled for a third son. She was a beauty, even today years later, but her mean nature added years to her face.

The note of censure in her voice could not be missed. A snob of the first order, Prudence had thought she missed out on the earldom by marrying a younger son. Victoria finished pouring the tea and schooled her features before turning around to face her.

"Her father was, although she was raised in York. From what Colleen has told me, her parents married against the wishes of both their families. They've had little or no contact with them. Even when she found herself alone and handling a small farm, she didn't go to them. Partially because she doesn't know where to look, but I think if she did, she wouldn't."

"What kind of woman would do such a thing?"

"A strong one," Anna piped in. Victoria had to bite her lip to keep from smiling.

"Well, if she trapped him into marriage—"

"Let us have one understanding. Colleen is my daughter-in-law. She's the new Countess of Penwyth. In this we will agree, particularly in public. With the rumors surrounding Sebastian's first marriage and those surrounding the recent...accidents...we need to present a united front. Do I make myself clear?"

Prudence's eyes rounded and she nodded. Victoria should have felt guilty, but she had to protect Sebastian and the title. Colleen was perfect for her arrogant son. With her quick wit and fiery temper, Victoria knew Sebastian wouldn't be able to ignore his wife. And with a little push in the right direction, she would be a grandmother within a year.

CRCBCR

Sebastian studied Colleen's features while she lay on the bed. She had not kept a bite of food down for three days running, which had drained her energy. She was pale, almost too pale, making the freckles on her nose even more prominent.

He caressed her cheek with the back of his fingers. With everything that had happened, he'd insisted they leave York immediately. He'd had no choice. It had been several weeks since his cousin's death, and he needed to be in London to take up the reigns. But, he regretted having to make the hasty trip. This had not been easy for her. She wrinkled her nose as he continued to touch her cheek. He chuckled at her expression.

She stirred and opened her eyes slowly. As always, the impact of those clear grey eyes staring straight at him left him slightly uncomfortable. It was as if she could see straight into his soul. Then she squinted.

"Where are my spectacles?" she asked. No "thank you" for dragging her up the stairs and taking care of her.

He reached into his breast pocket to retrieve them.

"Here." He handed them to her. She donned them but kept silent, blinking owlishly as her gaze focused. "You are welcome."

She struggled to sit up, and he grabbed a pillow and slid it behind her back. "There's no reason to get testy with me, my lord. I'm tired and actually hungry and not at all happy about my situation."

Irritation crawled down his spine. Would the woman never let go of it?

"Listen, I've had enough to handle the past few days without having to listen to you complaining about *your* situation."

"And I'm supposed to be happy with being uprooted from everything I know, everything I love, to live in a house of strangers?"

Her bottom lip quivered and he softened. With the pressures of his new title, he had forgotten everything she'd been through. "Colleen, we need to come to some kind of understanding."

She crossed her arms beneath her breasts. "The only thing I understand is that you lied. And if you think I am ever going to have any kind of marital relations with you...well, think again."

All those warm, soft feelings evaporated. He would never force a woman, but the fact that his wife acted as if she would rather die than consummate their union angered him. He'd survived one marriage like that. He would not endure another. He stepped closer and leaned over her, placing a fisted hand on each side of her on the bed. It was best that she faced facts. "Let us get one thing straight, *my lady*. You have exactly a week, one week, to prepare yourself for those so-called marital relations."

With that, he straightened and strode out of the room, slamming the door behind him.

Chapter Eight

Colleen raised a shaky hand and brushed a strand of hair out of her face. She glanced around, studying her surroundings. The bed was the biggest she'd ever seen, complete with a canopy and frilly bedclothes. The rest of the room was almost as big as her cottage. A warm fire crackled in the fireplace, and the furniture situated throughout the room was of a quality much better than she had ever seen, with various rugs covering the floor.

Instantly, she was ashamed for snapping at Sebastian. She'd never seen him in a temper before. She'd seen him irritated, drunk, childish and kind. Oh so very kind. His gentle ministrations during her illness had been a surprise. It had left her agitated and confused.

People were supposed to stay the way they were. Their personalities didn't change. Sebastian, *her husband,* was a rake of the worst kind. Women every night of the week, a flirt and a drunk and most assuredly a gambler. She sighed. She was blowing things out of proportion. Sebastian may be a rake, but he said he wasn't a drunk, and she noted he hadn't had a sip of liquor on their trip. And the gambling, well, if he did, he knew when to stop. But the flirting...

She was now married to a man who could have any woman in London, and he was not particularly attracted to her. But there had been a tenderness when he cared for her that left her with a flutter in her stomach.

But of course, they arrived in London, and he was back to acting the boor.

She sighed again. Her stomach grumbled and she decided to clean up. For the first time in three long days, she was actually hungry.

She stood. Her head spun and her stomach pitched. When her knees began to shake, she sank down on the bed again. Closing her eyes, she breathed deeply.

"My lady? Are you feeling all right?"

Colleen opened her eyes to find a young woman, dressed in a maid's outfit, standing at the threshold of her room.

"Just a little dizzy."

"My name's Sally. Lord Penwyth sent me to help you change and refresh yourself."

"Oh, but..." Colleen was unaccustomed to having someone help her dress. All of her dresses were made to be easily removed like most women of her station.

Most women of her station.

But she wasn't of that class anymore. Something in her stomach twisted and pitched. Lord, how had she gotten into such a mess?

"Lord Penwyth is sending some water up so you can bathe." Sally gently took Colleen's arm and helped her to her feet. Her face heated when her stomach grumbled.

"I'd planned on joining the others to eat."

As Sally helped her out of her dress, another wave of embarrassment engulfed Colleen. Other than her mother and sister, no other person, male or female, had seen her undressed. Sally either didn't recognize or care about her embarrassment. She continued talking as if it were an everyday occurrence for her.

"Lord Penwyth is having a tray readied and will join you. He says he wants you to rest."

Sally said it with such undisguised reverence and admiration, Colleen was immediately wary. The girl was in her early twenties, if Colleen guessed right, with a rounded figure and pretty blue eyes. Although she wouldn't have suspected it of him...

"Have you known Lord Penwyth very long?"

Before Sally could answer there was a knock at the door.

"That will be the water and tub." She guided Colleen, dressed only in her threadbare shift, behind a dressing screen. The next few minutes were filled with the sounds of the footmen bringing in the tub and loading it with water. As soon as the door closed, Sally's pretty face peeped around the side of the screen.

"This way, my lady."

Within moments, Colleen was completely naked, much to her embarrassment, although she tried her best not to let Sally know.

The maid helped Colleen into the tub. Her glasses fogged from the steamy water. Her skin warmed, and the tension drained from her muscles as did the ache in her head.

She closed her eyes and rested against the edge. Her earlier conversation with Sally nudged at her memory.

"Sally?"

"Yes, my lady?"

"Have you known Seb...er Lord Penwyth very long?" She winced at her attempt to sound casual.

"Yes, my lady." Without opening her eyes, Colleen knew the girl was smiling. She could hear it in her voice. "I grew up in his lordship's house. My mum is the housekeeper there."

"Oh," Colleen said, not knowing what else to say.

"Are you ready to get out, my lady?"

She nodded, still uncomfortable with the title and her nudity. Moments later, she was settled in a chair in front of the fireplace drying her hair and dressed in a borrowed wrapper. All the while, Sally continued a one-sided conversation.

"Lord Penwyth always says that he knew me before I was born, he does."

"Knew you before you were born?"

"Telling all my secrets, Sally?" Sebastian asked, his voice laced with amusement.

Colleen turned, and that funny little butterfly was back again. Casually, full of masculine pride and splendor, he walked into the room, a tray of food in his hands.

"Oh, no, Lord Penwyth. Just telling Lady Penwyth you've known me all me life."

His blue eyes sparkled as he smiled at the girl. "That I have. I think I can handle things from here, Sally."

She bobbed a curtsy and scurried out of the room. Sebastian set the tray on a table to Colleen's right and stood back to study her.

"You look a little better. Did the bath help?"

His voice was solicitous, his manners impeccable and his smile full of warmth. She didn't trust him. "Yes. Much better. I didn't need a maid, though. I am quite accustomed to taking care of my own needs."

"Good. Now, I convinced the cook to make you a wondrous sample of her good food. She makes the most unbelievable sticky buns, but alas, she didn't have any. I also brought some tea."

The aroma of the food reached her and she almost swooned. She was starving and thankful to finally have her appetite back. "That sounds wonderful, my lord."

He chuckled and fixed her a plate. "How very proper of you, my lady."

He handed her the plate and then fixed one for himself. As he sat in the chair opposite of hers, she tried to concentrate on her food and not the way the buckskin pants molded to his thighs. She took a sip of tea and almost choked. Good night, why did this man always make her behave and think like a hussy?

"Are you okay, Colleen?" He rose as if to help, but she motioned him to sit.

"I'm fine. Just went down the wrong way."

An uncomfortable silence settled between the two of them. Nothing but the crackle of the fire and the ticking of the clock on the mantle above it. She continued to eat and realized that maybe she was the only one discomforted by the lack of conversation. Sebastian was eating his food as if it were his last meal. Nothing bothered that man's appetite.

She had to think of something to break the silence. "How is the rest of the family?"

"Aunt Millicent is...still overcoming what has happened. It has all been a terrible experience for her."

"I can imagine. Were there any daughters?"

"Yes, four. Jocelyn, who has been married for several years, and Adele, who is twenty, married just under a year. Violet and Samantha are still in the schoolroom."

Five children. "Large family."

He smiled. "Yes, we do tend to have large families. I probably would have had more siblings, but Mother and Father were never blessed after Anna. And truthfully, after her, I'm sure they didn't have the energy."

They shared a smile. His eyes flashed with humor as they always did when he talked of his sister.

Her stomach flip-flopped again and a burst of warmth flashed through her. She shifted in her chair, mortified that the heat pooled in her belly had dipped down lower.

"Now the title is yours."

The humor faded from his eyes, and she almost regretted the comment. But without that warm look, she was safe. It was better to have distance. Only now, she wanted to rise from her chair and rush to his side to comfort him.

"Yes. I never thought I would...I was sure I would never hold the responsibility. Thankfully, my uncle taught me a lot about estate management as I had one of my own. My father left me with a massive estate in Hampshire."

Two estates.

She must have shown her dismay. "Don't worry, Colleen, we'll rub together well enough."

She nodded, and he filled their teacups again. Soon her eyes grew heavy and she lost the energy to eat.

"Are you ready for bed?"

"Yes."

He took her plate, setting it on the tray. When she tried to stand her legs wobbled and her head spun again.

"Slow down. I'll help you."

He lifted her into his arms and carried her to the bed. He laid her down gently and removed her spectacles. She whispered a thank you before drifting off to sleep.

CRCBCR

Sebastian studied his wife's face noting the dark smudges beneath her eyes had grown darker, but there was a flush to her cheeks he hadn't seen in three days. He brushed her cheek with the back of his fingers.

So soft.

A sliver of guilt wormed into his stomach. Rubbing his hand over the spot, he thought about his ultimatum earlier. He should have never threatened her like that. Granted, she had a way of slipping under his skin and scratching that sensitive surface. A part of him understood that the situation they were in was causing some of his annoyance—not to mention the added worry of his new role. But another part, a huge part, was due to his aggravation with her, wanting her the way he did. It was confusing, irritating and downright frustrating. The fact that she seemed to dismiss him so easily spurred his temper.

From the time he turned fourteen, Sebastian had women at his mercy. Even as a son of a second son, he had money and a position in society which attracted many. They came to him; he did not pursue. Even his duplicitous wife had originally been the aggressor. But—this woman—this *wife* not only didn't want him, he was positive she would be happier back in her dismal little cottage in York.

She sighed and shifted her weight until she rested on her side. Her wrapper fell open, revealing her satiny ivory skin. His blood heated and his groin tightened. Waiting to consummate their marriage was probably going to do him in. But the desire to have her, to be the first to touch her, almost overwhelmed him. The wave of possessiveness left him stunned. Even with his first wife, he'd never felt the need to protect, to own. This spinster with her spectacles and her ugly clothes caused feelings to rise he had no intention of dealing with.

He curled his fingers and stepped back from the bed, from temptation. They would consummate this marriage, they would have heirs, but he refused to lose himself in a woman. He'd made that mistake once and would not involve his heart again.

CRCBCR

Refreshed from a warm bath and some good brandy, Sebastian headed downstairs after checking on Colleen once more. He'd found her sound asleep, a little snore escaping every few seconds. His lips kicked up a notch. Wouldn't Colleen be upset to hear that?

When he reached the bottom of the stairs, Fitzgerald approached him.

"Sir, there is a *visitor* who *insisted* on seeing you. I explained you just arrived, but he would not leave. I've placed him in the library."

"Visitor? Anyone I know?"

"No, I would say not, my lord. But he knew the last Lord Penwyth."

"Uncle Albert?"

"No, my lord. Your cousin—"

"Gilbert."

Remorse filled him again. He still couldn't fathom losing both of them without knowing, never getting to say goodbye. He swallowed, trying to compose himself.

"Thank you, Fitzgerald. Don't disturb us unless it is absolutely necessary."

"Yes, my lord."

Sebastian walked down the hall, past the parlor that was now empty, his mother and sister probably resting in their rooms. As he approached the door to the library, his palms began to sweat. This was his first time acting as Earl Penwyth.

Without hesitating, he opened the door to find a rather tall, muscular fellow studying a row of books. His hair was short and combed. His dress was clean but not of the best material. He turned as soon as Sebastian stepped into the room, and he was pinned with a pair of dark brown eyes.

"You must be Lord Penwyth. The *new* Lord Penwyth," he said, his gravelly voice filled with suspicion.

Irritation and indignation filled Sebastian's gut. He may not have expected the position, but by damn this man would show a little more respect.

"Who may I ask are you?"

The man chuckled and walked forward. "You remind me a lot of the last Lord Penwyth. He talked of you often. My name is Michael Jenkins."

There was a hint of Scot in his voice. It reminded Sebastian of Colleen. "And Mr. Jenkins, what was the nature of your relationship with my cousin?"

"I'm a Bow Street Runner, my lord."

"A runner?" A myriad of scenarios flashed through his mind. But he couldn't think of a reason Gilbert, a studious man who could be trusted with a secret but would cheat you at cards with a smile and a quick hand, would need a runner.

"Why?"

"Why would someone like him need a runner?" Jenkins asked with a self-depreciating smile. "According to him, someone was trying to kill him."

Chapter Nine

The ticking of the clock was the only sound in the library as Sebastian studied his guest, Mr. Jenkins.

"Gilbert thought someone was trying to kill him?" he asked as he rounded the corner of his desk. He had to sit. His knees were threatening to give way, and he didn't want to embarrass himself.

"Yes, sir. In fact, he was positive his father had been murdered also."

"Any suspects?"

"You were number one on my list."

Irritation lanced through Sebastian. "I had no reason to kill my uncle or my cousin."

"Other than the title," Jenkins said with a sarcastic smirk on his face.

"I didn't want the title."

"Yes, he said as much. In addition, there is your trip to the continent, and then your injury in York that convinced me otherwise."

"Really?" Sebastian couldn't keep the lethal tone from his voice. He had been accused of many things in his life, a rake, a drunk, but never...

"Yes. You could have easily hired someone to do the job, but I have a feeling your situation up north was an attack on you. One by one, the heirs of Penwyth have been meeting with unfortunate *accidents*."

"You think both of them were murdered?"

"I have no proof. But I do have an uncle in peak physical condition who suddenly drops dead, a cousin who is deathly afraid of heights who falls to his death, and you're hit on the head and left for dead in the snow."

Gilbert's fear of heights was well known within the family. As boys, they had teased him constantly about it. He avoided anything past the second floor, and if he did need to be on the higher floors, he never approached the windows.

"And you suspected me?"

"You were my first suspect. Lord Penwyth was convinced you didn't want the title. In fact, he remembered you saying you were happy when he married."

"And that convinced you?"

Jenkins smiled without a trace of humor. "No. See, most murders are not done by strangers. Oftentimes, it is a member of the family, especially with an earldom at stake."

"What changed your mind?"

"You were injured, if my sources are correct."

No one but family knew about his accident. And other than Colleen, no one really knew just how close he came to dying.

"Ah, trying to sort it out? Well, you sent word of your return, where you were at the time, and all that. Servants gossip, my lord. Not viciously in this case, but this house is on edge with everything that has happened."

Sebastian could believe that. The majority of these servants had served the Penwyth estate most of their lives. Two accidental deaths and a missing heir would send some, if not all of them into a state of worry.

"Any other suspects?"

"Several. Of course, there is the line of the earldom. Your heir, your uncle, James Ware..."

"James." The name slipped off Sebastian's lips as he remembered the uncle he barely knew. Much younger than his two brothers and from his grandfather's second wife. A woman, who once his grandfather had died, had behaved like his own dear wife, with the morals of an alley cat.

"Yes, James. He does have an alibi for every incident, including yours."

"So you don't think it was him."

He didn't answer immediately, then said, "No, what I said was he had an alibi. But that doesn't mean he's not a suspect."

"Explain." It wasn't a question, but a command. Irritation burned in his belly.

"You were still considered a person of interest when you were on the continent. You have money, and that is a motivator to some of the more unsavory elements of our society," Jenkins remarked.

"You don't think it was for the money?"

"No, all of you, through your grandfather's good foresight, have money and estates to run. Your father, as did your uncle, worked hard on the estates, and their wealth grew. James accomplished neither."

"Are you telling me he's under the hatches?"

"No, he does well enough, although there are some indications he has a gambling problem. The motivator in this case, as I said, sir, is the title. And he has a daughter in her third season, with no offer in sight." Jenkins' voice had risen with his agitation.

"The title? You think that my uncle killed his brother and nephew all for a title? Then had someone attack me? That's insane."

"Yes. In my opinion. But some people revere a title more than wealth, more than happiness."

"What do you want from me?"

"I thought I should warn you. When your cousin first called on me, I didn't believe him. Thought he had an overactive imagination. Young lord, just lost his father, the mind can play tricks on a man who has a lot of time on his hands. But as I dug deeper, my instincts told me that there is something there. Someone is killing off the Earls of Penwyth. And in my opinion, you're the next in line to die."

C8C8C8

Silk sheets slid over her skin as Colleen turned over on her back. *Silk sheets?* Her eyes shot open, panic cramping her stomach. She squinted but couldn't make out the room. She wiggled to the edge of the bed, found a nightstand then her spectacles. She donned them, and when she was finally able to see, looked around the room. She was home, but she wasn't. Her new home was one of silks and fine china, of priceless vases and expensive furnishings. Of a husband who sent her pulse racing.

Where had that thought come from?

Truth was she felt like an imposter. She was the Countess of Penwyth, and she was a fraud. She longed for her tiny cottage with the smell of baked bread. She didn't want fine things, or a husband who didn't want her in return.

She sighed. Weak winter sunlight streamed through the window, casting shadows around the room. She swung her legs over the edge of the bed and stood only to have them buckle beneath her. She grabbed onto the mattress and eased step by step to the bedpost. Her legs shook with each step, her head whirling.

"What the bloody hell do you think you're doing?"

She winced at Sebastian's harsh tone. Then irritation and anger rode high. She glanced over her shoulder as he approached.

"Trying to escape," she said, knowing she sounded like a small child.

"Here, let me help you." His voice was full of aggravated male. He grabbed her by the waist and hoisted her in his arms. "What are you about?"

"I was going to walk to the chair," she said, pointing in the direction of where they had sat when they shared their meal.

He switched direction and gently placed her in the chair.

"I'm not an invalid, you know."

He sighed. "No, but you are still weak. I'm sure you'll be full of insults tomorrow."

She looked up at him as he stared down at her with narrowed eyes. "What?"

"You don't look well. In fact, if I didn't know better, I'd say you were at death's door. You're too pale, and you've dark circles under your eyes."

"Oh, my lord earl, you know how to romance a woman." The sarcasm dripped from her words. She couldn't help it. Even though she knew she shouldn't care, the fact that he found her lacking hurt.

He threw back his head and let go of a laugh that bounced off the walls of the room. She stared at him, transfixed by the sight. His usual cool mask had disappeared. He was replaced by a man so charming, so completely free, she blinked at the transformation.

When he stopped laughing, he focused on her and his lips curved seductively. Her heart slammed against her chest, and she had to look away. His blue eyes sparkling with humor sent a shiver of something she couldn't define sliding through her system, leaving her lightheaded. "I can always count on you, *my lady*, to put me in my place."

She ignored the curious warmth that curled in her belly when he called her my lady. She didn't want to be his lady. She didn't want to be *anyone's* lady.

"I have no doubt you will have much more interesting insults tomorrow." He stretched out his long legs, brushing the bottom of her wrapper with the tops of his boots. She moved her feet. "Now, I wanted to warn you. Mother is insisting on a trip to the modiste's tomorrow. If you don't feel well enough, tell her. She'll complain, but in the end she'll understand."

There was a knock at the door. Sebastian bid them to come in. A footman entered holding another tray laden with food.

"Thank you, Stephen," Sebastian said. "I took the liberty of having your meal arranged for you."

Stephen, a young man with light hair and a ruddy complexion, placed the tray on the table beside her.

"Thank you," she said.

He hurried out the door.

"You are not going to complain about my highhandedness?" Sebastian asked, his voice infused with laughter.

"I'm really too tired to bother," she replied smartly as she filled her plate. Then she shot him a smile. "I'm also hungry."

He chuckled. "One of these days that sarcasm is going to get you into trouble."

"Hmm. Aren't you going to eat?"

"No. I'm going to my club later. But I wanted to make sure you were attended to."

She just bet he was heading to his club. He probably intended to spend the evening with a ladybird in a cozy little property. She looked down at her plate and applied herself to eating. She couldn't fight the irritating feeling he was deserting her. He'd brought her to the capital, and now he planned on running off to have fun with some beautiful woman. Why, they hadn't even been in the capital for a day, and he was already forsaking his marriage vows. She swallowed her comments, knowing she had no right to question and definitely no right to judge him. Good night, she barely knew the man.

The emotion burning in her chest caused her appetite to sour. She sipped a bit of tea and thought about it. Why was she so upset that he was going out tonight? She should be happy he was leaving her alone. That's what she wanted, wasn't it?

The thought of Sebastian with his arms wrapped around another woman sent a searing heat of anger rolling through her. She blinked as she tried to swallow her food. She wasn't jealous, was she? No, there was no way she could be jealous of a woman who had to endure Sebastian's company.

Her appetite now completely dissolved, she said, "I guess I am not as hungry as I thought."

She couldn't meet his eyes, but the whisper of his concerned gaze sent a vibration down her spine. He helped her back to bed, pulling the covers to her chin as if she were a child.

"Get some rest, Colleen." His voice was absolute. She glanced up and had to look away. The worry in his eyes bothered her and made her feel comforted at the same time. Before Sebastian, it had been so long since she'd been cared for. It was disconcerting how much she yearned for his attention.

He was out the door a second later, and she was left to ponder her disturbing thoughts.

CRCBCR

Victoria sipped her tea, laced with a heavy dose of brandy, in the privacy of her sitting room. It had been a long trip home. Sighing in contentment, she closed her eyes and thought of her daughter-in-law. There was something so familiar about Colleen. Her eyes had struck Victoria from the moment they met. Grey, no hint of blue, very unusual.

Her mind drifted back thirty years to her first few years of marriage. She'd been so happy, so thrilled to have married the man she loved. A memory she'd forgotten rose, of a young woman, the granddaughter of a duke. The young girl had been considered the catch of the season and should have been having the time of her life. But there was a sadness about her, something Victoria realized many people didn't see. Didn't want to see. The ton liked their entertainment, and they wanted their Incomparable of the Season to adhere to their ideal.

Again, the image of the woman flashed across Victoria's mind. Impeccably dressed, statuesque, demure, all of these described the woman, but the thing that Victoria always noted when she saw the other woman was bone-deep sorrow in her eyes. Victoria's own eyes snapped open; her heartbeat sped up a beat or two when she thought of the color of the sad woman's eyes. Clear, cool grey, fringed with dark lashes, so like Colleen's.

Her mind twisted through the memories, trying to remember the woman's name, trying to remember what happened to her. It had been a simple name, something... *Jane*...that was it. She remembered there had been some kind of a scandal attached to her. Scores of men had been attracted to her, not just because of her position as a duke's granddaughter, but because of her beauty, her poise. There had been rumors hinting that she'd received at least a half a dozen proposals, all of which she had refused. A duke's son had offered, but she had turned him down. Her father had thrown a fit. *What was her father's name?*

Duke of Ethingham. She had forgotten about the old bastard. And for good reason. The man was an excellent example of a lazy aristocrat. Word was he had peculiar tastes, especially for inflicting pain and for young girls. Victoria shivered. He'd died several years later, killed in a duel.

The young woman's father had insisted on the match, or at least that is what everyone had said. But the scandal had involved another young man, Scottish, the younger son of a laird...they had run off together.

Now, Victoria just had to come up with a plan to discover if her theory was right or not.

CR CB CR

Upon entering his club, Sebastian claimed a seat next to a blazing fire. It had been over nine months since he'd entered White's, and after dealing with women for the past six days, he needed a break. He took a healthy swig of brandy and allowed it to seep into his muscles and relax him.

"Ho, Sebastian," a voice bellowed from behind him. "When did you get back into town?"

He turned and watched as Daniel, Earl of Bridgerton, walked across the room. Only an inch shorter than he, Daniel contrasted him in looks with light brown hair and golden brown eyes. Many matchmaking mamas wanted their daughter to be the man's countess, much to Daniel's irritation. Even with his reputation, most of it deserved, debutantes tried their best to capture his attention. As far as Sebastian knew, Daniel still swore to never marry.

His best friend since their salad days, Daniel was treated as a member of Sebastian's family. His life at home had not been good, and he had spent most holidays at school until Sebastian's mother had discovered what was going on. After that, he had been a regular at every holiday event.

He rose and accepted Daniel's hand. After they were seated, Daniel came right to the point. "Did your ninny of a sister and your mother find you?"

"Yes, they did. I was in York when they finally found me."

"Ah. They lost the men I had following them just outside of London. I guess they told you about the whole mess?" He sighed. "Shame really. Liked your uncle and your cousin."

Sebastian nodded. "Both damn fine men and best of friends. Hard to believe they are gone."

As if knowing Sebastian's mood was quickly turning sour, Daniel changed the subject. "So how does it feel to be an earl now? The matchmaking mamas are all atwitter over rumors of your return. They assume you are going to marry to beget an heir."

Sebastian smiled. "That won't be necessary."

"It won't? Can't see that you would want the title to go to that skinflint of an uncle and his wife." Daniel shuddered theatrically, and Sebastian laughed. "I almost feel sorry for that dowdy little cousin of yours... What is her name?"

"Cicely." He thought about the quiet girl he'd met a handful of times and her overbearing mother and absent father. "James and Prudence must be nightmare parents."

Daniel took a healthy swig of his brandy when Sebastian made his next statement.

"That won't happen. You see, I've found myself a wife."

Daniel choked on his drink. "A wife? You're getting married?"

"I *am* married."

Daniel's gaze sharpened as he studied him, but Sebastian just smiled smugly.

"I think we should retire to my house, and I expect the entire story, Sebastian."

A half hour later, he followed Daniel into his library. "Now, tell me about this woman you have married. Is there a way out of it?"

He watched Daniel pour two glasses of brandy. After witnessing what Sebastian's marriage did to him, Daniel had sworn never to repeat the mistake. Sebastian had made the same pledge, but here he was, married to a woman he barely knew.

"I'm not sure I want a way out of it," Sebastian said as he settled in a chair. "The woman saved my life and I ruined her reputation."

"She trapped you?" Suspicion colored his voice.

Sebastian chuckled. "She's not that thrilled about being married to me. It all started at Crammer's house party."

As Daniel listened to the story, his eyes grew wider and more concerned. "Is the marriage legal?"

"Do you mean is there a possible way to relieve myself of my wife?"

Daniel nodded.

"I am sure there would be if I protested it. But it was all done legally, under the vicar, with a special license. And besides, I could not leave the woman after her reputation had been ruined, thanks to saving my life."

After a few minutes of silence, Daniel sighed. "You're telling me someone knocked you on the head, doused you with whiskey and left you to die?"

"Yes, and if she hadn't found me, I would surely be dead."

In a quiet voice, Daniel said, "Given what's happened recently, I would have to say that was someone's plan."

Chapter Ten

Sebastian didn't say a word for several seconds and allowed Daniel's suspicions to sink in. The first thing he felt was relief. He'd been so sure he was losing his mind with all the ideas of assassins and conspiracies floating around.

"Do you think this new wife of yours could be part of the plan?" Daniel asked.

Sebastian chuckled, thinking of the verbal lashing Colleen would give Daniel for that accusation. "No, I told you she saved my life. On top of that, she doesn't have a dishonest bone in her body."

Daniel's eyes narrowed. "Really?"

"Yes, really. I'm not losing my mind here, and truthfully, being married to a woman with no connections, no dowry and no personality, doesn't appeal. But I owed the woman. Why would she save my life if she were part of the plan?"

Daniel settled back in his chair, a frown creasing his forehead. "Well, then, if the runner you told me about believes that your cousin and uncle were murdered, and now the killer is after you, it has to be someone in line for the earldom."

"James."

"Uncle James. That man always made me uncomfortable. He has those beady little eyes."

Sebastian laughed. "I know what you mean. He was always an outsider. But I can't see that he would be after the earldom. Silly in my opinion."

It was Daniel's turn to chuckle. "No, you wouldn't, but men have been killed over lesser titles. The title, money and land; that would be more than enough to tempt some. Of course, you will have another worry. Once whoever is after your title finds out you've married, you will not be the only target."

"And why, pray tell, would my wife be a target? That is, assuming you are referring to my new bride."

"Think, Sebastian. Any heir would keep whoever wants the title from having it. And he would have to wait until at least three or four months after your demise to ensure she wasn't breeding, to gain the title."

"Hmmm," was all Sebastian could say. Mainly because his thoughts had turned to Colleen and begetting heirs. He knew he could tame the woman. When they had kissed, he felt her underlying passion, something shimmering below the surface. She kept it well hidden from the rest of the world, but he knew he could unlock it and reap the rewards.

Just thinking about his wife and her passion had sent all of his blood out of his head rushing straight to his groin. He stifled a groan and shifted in his chair, trying to relieve the pressure.

"Ah, so I guess the killer would have to worry about your heirs?" Daniel asked, one eyebrow raised in question.

"No, not yet. But..." The image of Colleen with her soft curves and warm flesh materialized. The pressure intensified.

Sebastian gulped down the remainder of his brandy and rose to fill the glass again. It was going to be a long few nights until he could unleash Colleen's inner passion. He needed something to take his mind off his wife, he thought as he drank down more brandy.

CRCBCR

"Jameson, I can undressh myshelf," Sebastian slurred loud enough for everyone on Curzon Street to hear.

Colleen opened her eyes, her husband's voice bringing her out of a sound sleep. She sat up, testing her body. No more dizziness and just a few aches. She grabbed her spectacles off her nightstand and donned them and her wrapper. She rose out of bed and crept to the door she assumed connected her chamber to her husband's room.

"I'll tell you when I want some help from you, Jameson. This ish not one of those times."

Jameson's "Yes, my lord" was barely audible.

The door opened then closed, telling Colleen that her husband must be alone. She waited, wondering if she should interrupt him to make sure he could make it to bed.

"Bloody hell!" he yelled, which was followed by the sound of a large body falling to the floor. Colleen threw the door open and rushed into the room to find her husband in much the same condition as she had found him that very first time. Laid out flat on the floor. Only this time he was fully awake, a sloppy drunken grin on his face.

Impatience and resentment sped through her. Not twenty-four hours in London, and the idiot was drunk as a sailor.

"Ahhh, wife. I see that you have rushed to my rescue again. I can't seem to get the other sleeve off."

It was then that she realized Sebastian was bare-chested, one arm still tangled in the sleeve. She hadn't seen him like this since she had nursed him back to health, and he had been incoherent at the time. But as he struggled with his sleeve, she couldn't take her eyes off the great expanse of golden skin before her.

He should look ridiculous, fighting with his linen shirt for freedom. But for some reason, Colleen found herself a bit more entranced by the sight. She didn't know if it was the boyish frown on his sensuous lips or the tingle of warmth chasing down her spine as she gazed at his chest. Either way, she couldn't prevent the laugh that bubbled up.

He stopped his struggles and stared at her with such an intensity all the breath tangled in her throat, and her laughter died.

"You should do that more often." His lips curved and his eyes darkened. "I don't believe I've ever heard you laugh before, not like that." Then he shook his head. "No, once. Once I heard you laugh like that."

She shifted from foot to foot. Uncomfortable with the warmth spreading into her belly at the sound of his deepened voice and frank appraisal, she lashed out, "I don't have much to laugh about, do I, my lord?"

Instead of pulling back from her as she had intended, his eyes warmed. "You've had a hard life, haven't you?"

"I have no idea what you are talking about." Her voice was stiff as was her spine. Standing next to the bed, with Sebastian sitting on the floor half-naked, was not good for her composure. She was trying not to stare at him, especially the way his copper nipples had puckered against the chill in the room.

"You're an orphan, and your sister died last year. You're alone in the world."

"I'm not an orphan." She bit off each word. Mortification that he pitied her caused her tone to sharpen. "I was practically an adult by the time my mother passed on. And I'm married to you, so I am not alone in the world."

Why she added that last bit of information she did not know, but regretted it the moment his lips curved and a dangerous glint flashed in his eyes.

"Of course, you have me." He placed his free hand on the bed and hoisted himself off the floor.

Suddenly, he was no longer the drunken rogue but something much more dangerous. He'd moved so close, the very heat of him warmed her. She took a step back.

His shirt still dangled from one arm, his smile turned completely seductive and his eyes darkened to cobalt. He took a step forward. His bay-rum scent, mixed with the scent of brandy, surrounded her, seduced her.

"You know, Colleen, you look rather fetching in that gown."

Her stomach clenched at the sloppy compliment. A whisper of need crawled into her heart and she pushed it away. She wouldn't fall for a charmer. In the end, she would be left lonely by a man who found solace with other women. But even as she hardened her heart against him, she couldn't fight a smile as she watched him try to remove his shirt with the cufflink still fastened.

"Sebastian, you need to sit down and I'll help you. Why didn't you let Jameson help you?"

His whole body stilled. Colleen sensed that his every muscle was tensed and ready to pounce.

"Say that again."

"Why didn't you let—?"

"No, say my name. Say Sebastian."

The air between them thickened. She swallowed as she tried to calm her heart. The intensity in his eyes took her breath away. "Sebastian."

"I like it when you say my name." His voice had deepened, causing her blood to rush through her. It danced along her nerve endings and the tingling warmth in her belly now slid between her thighs.

"Sebastian," she said sharply.

He chuckled, and the sound of it vibrated across her senses. "Even when you sound like a prude you make me hard."

His blunt words should have embarrassed her or enraged her. Instead, a tiny zing of happiness shot through her blood. She tried her best to squelch her rising desire, but it was hard when a man like her husband admitted to his attraction to her.

"I can't seem to get this off." He was swinging his arm back and forth, still attempting to get his arm free of his shirt.

"Here. Sit on the bed, and I'll help."

Obediently he sat, his lips still curved into a smile so enticing she had to count backwards from ten trying to ignore it. Then count again.

"I never thought I'd hear you say those words, Colleen." The dip in his voice could only be termed flirtatious.

"Oh, shut up, you drunken sod," she said, attempting to disregard the flare of desire his words had caused.

She worked the gold cufflink free of its hole and yanked the shirt off him. Even in the dim candlelight, she could see his muscles flex beneath his golden skin each time he moved. She fought the urge to run her fingers over his muscled chest, to glide them over his warm skin.

"I'm going back to my room." She had to. He was entirely too attractive with his lips quirked in invitation and his chest bare for her hands to explore.

"But I need help with my pants."

She heard the amusement in his voice and suppressed a smile. She shouldn't be amused at his clumsy attempts at seduction, should she?

"Call Jameson." She turned to leave when his next statement stopped her.

"But I want you to help me, Colleen." His voice was such a mixture of petulant boy and seductive man that her traitorous heart softened.

She turned and found him sitting in the same spot, and although he still seemed amused, she sensed a deeper vibration between them. Something so strong it wiped every thought from her brain as she watched him raise his hand to her.

For a moment, she hesitated. She didn't know what he expected from her if she accepted that hand. Even as she yearned to lose herself in his warmth, she still had some concept she could convince him they needed to seek an annulment. For so many—too many—reasons she knew it was for the best. But freeing herself from his influence, and this attraction she had for him, would be the most important.

Never in her life had a man's smile twisted her insides and made her want something...more. The ache in her heart had started the day she found him, and it was growing every day. If she allowed him to ease the pain of loneliness she had fought for so many years, she didn't know if she would survive when he left.

"I don't bite unless asked." His teasing tone was almost her undoing. How long had it been since she'd had someone to share a jest with? She craved that as much as she craved his kisses. "I just need some help and then I'll leave you be. My fingers just don't seem to want to work."

It was a lie, she was sure of it. But the more she tried to keep her composure rigid, the more she found herself softening.

He would hurt her in the end. She knew it and he knew it. But in the dark, Colleen allowed the need she'd ignored most of her life to push her forward. She stepped closer and took his hand.

His breath escaped in a sigh, as if he had been worried she'd deny his request. His large, warm fingers wrapped around her hand.

"You're as cold as ice," he said, his voice now a whisper that stirred longings and desires she'd never known dwelled within her.

He pulled her closer, his hand still firmly gripping hers. He urged her into the vee of his legs. Her breasts, now level with his eyes, swelled and grew heavy, and her nipples tightened almost painfully.

"You need to stand so I can get your pants off you."

He chuckled again. "I'll let you in on a little secret, love. You don't have to be standing to do that."

The next instant, he tugged her onto the bed and rolled on top of her. His hardened body covered her from head to toe. His arousal pressed against her most private parts.

"Now, let's talk about your helping me with my pants."

Chapter Eleven

Sebastian closed his eyes. Every soft, wonderful curve Colleen possessed was plastered against him. Nothing in his life had felt quite so wonderful. He opened his eyes, reveling in the dark fire of her hair spread across the pristine white sheets.

So much hair. So many ideas.

He braced himself on his elbows on the bed, relieving her of his weight. Colleen was not a small woman, but she definitely was a woman. His hardened arousal was a testament. It took every bit of his willpower not to press his groin against her. From her wide-eyed expression, he would upset Colleen if he did that.

She swallowed and then licked her lips. The thought of kissing her lips, of tasting her there, of tasting her everywhere, sent most of his blood to his loins. He groaned, and her eyes grew larger, as if she were afraid of being ravished. Because, of course, she should be afraid. At the moment, his brain had stopped functioning. The only thing he could think about was sinking into her warmth and being lost.

"Sebastian?" A tremor of fear threaded her voice.

"Colleen, I'm not going to hurt you."

Even in the dim light, he could see the disbelief in her eyes. Her distrust, her wariness of men, was something he would have to overcome. *Patience.*

"All I want is a kiss, love."

Her lips parted, and he watched, fascinated by the pulse in her throat as her neck and face flushed. Ah, not that immune to him, was she?

His control threatened to crumble as the moist heat of her sex warmed him through their clothing. Good God, he hadn't even started, and she was responding. What did she hide under those prim clothes and pinched looks?

Unable to wait, to hold back any longer, he bent his head and took her lips. Not completely. Instead, he placed small kisses, just missing her mouth, a whisper of a caress guaranteed to drive them both mad.

He did not close his eyes. Rather, he left them open, staring into hers, which were luminous behind her spectacles, as he teased her mouth with his half kisses. Her breathing deepened, and a moment later her eyes slid closed.

Triumph pumped through him. He skimmed his hands up to cup her face. Her skin was so soft, so delicate. No longer able to restrain himself, he took complete possession of her mouth. She opened instantly to his questing tongue, and the taste of her exploded across his senses. Warm power flooded his body and he was lost to the moment.

Never in his life had a kiss been quite so erotic. Colleen's hands no longer lay limply by her side but tangled in his hair, her fingers digging into his scalp. He was fully on top of her, breast to chest, belly to belly, his hard member pressing against her soft core. He locked his jaw, trying to reign in his control and not embarrass himself for the first time since the age of sixteen.

He moved his hips, closing his eyes, reveling in the feel of her against him. She stilled and tried to pull her head away from him. But Sebastian held tight and kissed her while he continued moving. A second or two later, she softened and returned his kisses again.

The musky scent of her arousal filled the room, furthering his own. Nothing else mattered. The way they met and married, not to mention his distrust of women, all faded into the background. The need to make this woman his—his lover, his mate, his wife—surged within him, pounded in his heart and soul.

He shifted his weight and palmed her breast through the thin fabric of her wrapper and nightclothes. A few light touches and her nipple pebbled. He groaned. How had this woman hidden all this passion beneath her fussy exterior? He desired her now, wanted to take her as was his due as her husband, but knew he needed to proceed slowly. He pulled away, closed his eyes and took a ragged breath.

"Sebastian?" she asked, her voice breathless and worried.

He looked down at her. His heart stopped for a beat then slammed hard against his rib cage. Her glorious hair lay in disarray, her glasses fogged and her lips full and rosy from his kisses.

She shifted her lower body, unintentionally he was sure, causing her sex to press harder against him. The woman was going to kill him. He closed his eyes and shuddered.

"Sebastian?" Now her voice held a note of hurt. Every muscle in her body stiffened. "Don't worry. I understand. If you would just get up." The primness was back in her tone, and a hint of resignation colored it. Almost every ounce of his seductress had disappeared.

Before answering, he moved to cover her fully again. "Colleen, what is it you understand?"

The silvery depths of her eyes darkened. "I understand that our marriage is to be one of convenience."

"Convenience?" he muttered.

Through his irritation, her underlying tone reached him. He held his usually sharp tongue as he analyzed what lay behind the comment. Did he detect a note of disappointment? Was she regretting their marriage or her misassumption that it would be sexless? And with her response, she did desire him.

"Colleen, I have told you before, and I will tell you again, there is nothing convenient about our marriage."

Her eyes, already huge behind her spectacles, widened. Fire ignited in them, but not the kind he wanted.

Before she could open her mouth to argue, he swooped in for another kiss, moving against her. His blood shot to molten lava as she returned the kiss, shyly tangling her tongue with his.

He pulled back, both of them breathless. "I told you I never wanted another marriage, but I plan on claiming you as my wife, my *true* wife."

"But you don't—"

He flexed his hips again, stopping her protest. Her eyes fluttered closed. She sank her teeth into her bottom lip and hummed. The sound licked across his senses, bolstering his already runaway arousal.

"I don't what?" Even he heard the huskiness, the desire, in his voice. "Don't want you? Good God, woman, are you that naïve?"

Then the truth of it struck him. Of course she was. She was a virgin and a country-bred one at that. If he rushed things, she would never forgive him. Being a gentleman in his aroused state was going to kill him. He groaned and dropped his head to her shoulder. He would surely earn sainthood for this.

He raised his head and looked down at her. Her eyes were still closed as if waiting for her execution. For the first time in his life, Sebastian had to deal with a total innocent. For a sheltered woman like Colleen, sex probably frightened her and even though she might desire him, there was a good chance his passion would disgust her. He was harder than a steel saber, and the woman wanted nothing to do with him. That thought was enough to sober him.

"Colleen, I apologize for taking liberties. I...I had a bit too much to drink tonight, and I..." He what? Wanted to take her like a conquering Viking who thought it his right to rape and pillage? He was sure that would go over well with his bride.

He raised himself to his hands. Before he could move completely away from her, she twined her legs around his waist and wrapped her arms around his neck.

Her eyes were now open. The desire lighting them nearly had him losing control right then and there.

"Please, Sebastian."

With that quiet plea, full of timid arousal, all of his control broke. He groaned and gave her a quick, hard kiss. "Anything to please my wife."

She protested as he lifted away from her. "Love, I have to get these clothes off you before I go insane."

Her breathing hitched. "You...you want to see me naked?"

There it was, that damned doubt. True, she wasn't a diamond of the first water. No, her features were too prominent for that. And red hair and grey eyes weren't all the rage, he knew. But in his mind blonde hair and blue eyes were overrated. Especially now that he had seen Colleen's hair unbound and her eyes darkened with passion.

"Oh, yes, I want to see every glorious inch of your body naked."

She swallowed but didn't say a word, just watched him warily. He took that as her consent, and within moments, her wrapper lay on the floor. He untied the ribbons and pulled open the bodice of her modest gown as anticipation surged through him.

Every thought vanished when he revealed her breasts, bathed in candlelight. Pale ivory, smooth as silk, tipped with rosebud nipples. He brushed the back of his fingers against them, reveling in the hardened points. Her indrawn breath filled the silent room.

Without hesitation, he bent his head and took one turgid nipple into his mouth. The taste of her sent another wave of heat through him. So sweet...so delicious. He moved from one breast to the other, emboldened by her moans. Her fingers slid in his hair, urged him closer. That one little gesture sent a shock of conquest roaring through his blood. His control vanished as he gripped her nightgown, yanking it up over her head and throwing it on the floor behind him. The sight of her naked flesh momentarily stunned him.

Never in his life had a woman's body been so much of a surprise. Beneath the layers of prim and proper clothing lay a wonderland of soft, smooth skin. His gaze moved from her breasts, to her tiny waist and full hips, to the thatch of bright red hair between her legs. She shifted restlessly, but nothing deterred his study of her body, especially her legs.

Longer than any woman's legs he had ever seen, shapely, without being muscular. Oh, Jesus. The vision of having them wrapped around his waist sparked the already out-of-control fire within him.

He lay down next to her, resting on one elbow.

"Sebastian?"

"Yes, love?"

"What are you doing?"

He broke his gaze from her legs and refocused on her face. She stared at him as if he'd gone insane. And he was insane. Hot, greedy need licked at him, clawed at his senses. The urgency to claim her, to make her his, exploded in his blood. Not even with his first marriage when he had been so sure of his love had he wanted a woman this much.

"I'm trying to figure out just how long you've been hiding this wonderland beneath all that clothing."

He grazed one nipple with his fingers then continued down her rounded stomach and rested his palm on her sex. She shivered.

Damp heat warmed his hand. Closing his eyes, he drew in a deep breath and prayed for control. He slid one finger between her folds and wanted to shout when he found them slick with arousal.

She tensed the moment his finger entered her.

He leaned closer, his lips almost touching her ear. "It's okay, Colleen. I have to prepare your body for mine." He pulled her earlobe between his lips and sucked on it. Moving his finger, he spoke in low, soothing tones, trying to ease her tension.

"I'd rather you would just get it over with."

He chuckled. Normally the statement would have stopped him, but she'd delivered it in a voice husky with arousal. He said nothing more, just continued to move his finger, adding another. As he continued, her muscles relaxed and her hips began to shift. Soon, she planted her feet on the bed, moving with him. Her sweet honey drenched his hand. As her moans grew in volume, he pressed against her hardened nub and sent her shooting over the edge.

"Sebastian."

Her inner muscles locked on his fingers and the need for him to find his release within her overwhelmed any thoughts of holding back. He removed his hand from her flesh and grabbed the front of his trousers, ripping them open.

A moment later he was on top her, guiding his member inside of her. She clamped tight around him. "Colleen, look at me."

Her eyes slid open, sated passion darkening them.

"There is no going back." With that statement, he entered her fully, breaking past her maidenhead. Her swift intake of breath told him even though she had been prepared, it still had hurt.

"I'm sorry, love. There was no other way."

She nodded but said nothing. He closed his eyes, reveling in the feel of being inside of her. She was so tight he thought he would expire right there. He opened his eyes, rested his forehead against hers. Her grey eyes no longer held any hint of sensuality as they did before. He wanted to soothe her pain, so he pressed his lips to her forehead, then her nose, her mouth. A spike of relieved excitement spread through him when she opened without hesitation. His tongue stole inside for a taste.

He pulled back from the kiss and looked into her eyes. Knowing that there was nothing he could do to ease the pain, he pulled out and then sank back in. He balanced himself on his arms, continuing his motion. Several more thrusts and Colleen moved with him, matching his rhythm. Her throaty moans grew in volume, the sound pushing him to the pinnacle. Elation whipped through him as she moaned his name. He hoped the pain was a distant memory for her now and all she could feel was pleasure. His rhythm increased. She contracted around him. He thrust into her once more and her muscles pulled him deeper, milking his release from him.

Moments or maybe hours later, he moved to her side, drawing her against him. He drew in a deep breath, the scent of their lovemaking still ripe in the air, and looked down at Colleen. From her even breathing, Sebastian knew his wife had fallen asleep. And rightly so. After the tiring trip to London and now the bout of lovemaking, there was no doubt she was exhausted.

He couldn't stop the satisfied smile curving his lips. Never in his life would he have expected Colleen to be so sensual. As he thought of all the things he would love to teach her, he felt himself grow hard again, so he forced himself to think of other things. Taking her again was out of the question. She snuggled closer, her head upon his shoulder, her hand over his heart. Content, Sebastian joined his wife in slumber, not even realizing he gained more comfort from this closeness than he did making love.

CRCBCR

"When did he return?" he asked anxiously.

His partner settled in the high-backed chair behind the desk. The cloying scent of flowers permeated the air, and he fought not to cover his mouth to avoid the smell.

"This afternoon with a wife in tow."

A shiver of dread curdled his stomach contents. "I heard she's a bit dowdy. You know how Sebastian loves the beauties."

His partner snarled. "Do you think that matters? Now that he's earl he'll not want another scandal. He endured the embarrassment of being married to an alley cat the first time. Now, with this marriage, more is at stake. And if there is one thing Sebastian Ware knows, it's how to seduce a woman."

He eyed his partner, worried about the hysterical ranting. "Maybe he won't worry about that. You know him. He's a connoisseur of women."

"She is plain, but he will want to establish himself as earl, and what better way to do that than produce an heir."

Cold fear slithered down his spine. They were too close to lose it all.

His partner's eyes turned colder, more determined. "And you know what he's like. He'll sleep with just about anything in skirts."

He sighed. "So we have to do this quickly."

"Sebastian must die, and if not soon, that new little wife will have to go also."

Chapter Twelve

Colleen awoke with a start, her surroundings distorted without her spectacles. She knew one thing. This was *not* her room. She shifted, coming in contact with another person. A rather large person. Then, the events of the past few days flashed through her mind, most prominently, the night before. She closed her eyes in mortification. She had practically begged Sebastian to make love to her.

Slowly, and with special care as not to wake him, she moved to the edge of the bed and searched for her spectacles. She located them on the bedside table.

After donning them, she looked around the room and noticed the sun peeking through the heavy velvet drapes.

She stood and then shrieked, jumping back into bed when she realized she had not a stitch of clothing on.

"Good morning to you, love," Sebastian said, his voice husky with sleep and slightly amused.

She turned to find Sebastian sitting up in bed, his jaw littered with whiskers, his inky hair a mass of waves and his blue eyes twinkling at her.

She cleared her throat and clutched the sheets tighter.

"Good morning." She hoped her voice expressed an aura of nonchalance, but she knew she failed. Especially when she couldn't look him in the eye. She concentrated at a point over his shoulder, pretending she wasn't sitting next to him naked...while he was naked, too.

He chuckled. The rich, masculine sound crept down her spine. She shivered.

"Just how far does that blush go? Hmmm?" He chuckled and without warning, leaned forward and caressed her cheek with the back of his fingers. The unexpected touch caught her off guard. Her skin tingled along the path his fingers had taken. She looked at him.

"How are you this morning?" he asked.

The sound of his voice, infused with tenderness, caused her heart to jump. She fought the urge to lean into the caress, to gather strength from his touch.

"I'm fine," she said.

"Are you sure? I thought I might have been a little..." His voice trailed away. His eyes darkened and his breathing deepened.

"I'm fine, really, Sebastian." She bit her bottom lip nervously then licked it. She started when Sebastian groaned.

He abruptly pulled away from her and stood. Oblivious of his nudity, he stalked to the end of the bed, picked up a black silk robe and shrugged into it. She was held mesmerized by the play of his muscles as he moved. The man was all quiet control and strength. Through his actions, he continued to mutter. She couldn't quite make out what he was saying, but she figured it was directly related to her.

He sat beside her. She dropped her gaze to her lap, watching her hands as they twisted in the bedsheet. A few seconds of silence stretched between them. Even though she didn't look up, Colleen felt his gaze roaming over her. Heat warmed her face as the memories of his lovemaking washed over her.

"I'd pay a thousand pounds to know what caused that blush." Low, seductive, his voice caused her face to burn brighter.

"I'm so glad that you seem to think this is funny." Her tone was sharp with embarrassment and she almost regretted snapping at him. His smile slipped a bit but he carried on.

"I am sorry if you felt...pressured last night."

At first, she wondered what on earth he was referring to. Then she realized it was their lovemaking. By his serious tone and steady gaze, she knew he was worried that he had taken advantage. Learning he had a bit of a conscience lightened her mood.

She smiled, or tried to. "No, Sebastian, you didn't pressure me last night, it is just..."

He leaned forward, his whole body vibrating with tension. "It is just what?"

She pulled her bottom lip between her teeth and looked away. "I didn't think you would... Hmm..."

Silence stretched again and then he sighed. "Colleen."

She looked up. A gentle smile curved his lips, and his eyes lit with warmth. "You didn't think we would consummate?"

Swallowing, she said, "I didn't think you would want to."

His smile transformed into a grin, and her heart turned over. Sunlight streamed in behind him, highlighting his tousled locks. Even clothed in only a dressing gown, he exuded the air of a nobleman. He reached for one of her hands and inched closer, while he fought her grip on the sheet. When he finally untangled her fingers, he lifted her hand to his mouth, brushing his lips over her knuckles. She felt the whiskers on his chin against her skin.

"You thought I wouldn't want you. I think I proved that idea wrong." He curled her hand against his chest. Shifting closer, he leaned in and pressed his mouth against hers. "Colleen, you have to be the most idiotic woman I know."

She jerked her head away in surprise. "What do you mean by that?"

"How could you not know that—"

"I was a virgin, you lout. How was I supposed to know?"

He offered her a sheepish smile and started to lean closer again. This time, she settled back into the pillows. But when he was within an inch of her, his bedroom door swung open. He said something particularly nasty under his breath, but she heard him just the same and turned to look at who interrupted them. She sank lower, hiding behind him in embarrassment. She might be his wife, but she was his naked wife at the moment.

"Sebastian, dear, we can't seem to find Colleen." His mother's voice was loud and tinged with a shade of worry.

"It's all right, Mother." Humor laced his tone.

There was a rustle of silk and a flurry of footsteps. "This is not funny, Sebastian. We've been in London less than a day, and you have lost your wife." Her irritation rang clearly as she drew nearer to the bed. "Colleen is not a London miss. She is country bred and even after that horrific ride, I would think she would be up...oh."

"Oh, indeed, Mother."

Colleen pulled the sheet up over her head, still hiding behind Sebastian. She'd had enough humiliation in the last ten minutes to last a lifetime.

His mother cleared her throat. "Colleen, dear, we are going to shop after you are ready to go. And don't delay her, Sebastian."

"Would I do such a thing?"

"Oh, stop. I know you better than anyone. I will see you shortly, Colleen."

A few seconds later, Colleen heard the door close. The bed moved as Sebastian shifted back to face her.

"You can come out now."

Realizing she was still trying to hide behind him, she sat up, pulling the sheet down from in front of her face.

"You should have seen the expression on my mother's face. She was ready to do battle looking for you."

"I am sure this is an everyday occurrence in your life, my lord, but I hate to inform you it isn't for me. It isn't every day I find myself in a man's bedroom without a stitch of clothing on."

He placed a hand on either side of her hips, bringing his face closer. "Not just any man—your husband. And whether you like it or not—and after last night I would think I proved you did like it—there will be many mornings like this. Without the intrusion of my mother. At least, I hope so." He gaze dipped down to her breasts and he sighed. "She would kill me if I made you late. And you need a bath to relax."

Before she knew what he was about, he gave her a quick, hard kiss that made her toes curl and bounded off the bed.

"I'll get a warm bath sent up." He scooped up her wrapper and gown. After laying it at her feet, then backing away from the bed, he smiled. "I'll let you get dressed, and I will send up some food along with the bath."

With that, he walked into his dressing room. She slipped out of bed. After pulling on her gown and wrapper, she was at a loss of what to do. Should she go back to her room, or should she stay in his? Rubbing her temple, she tried to remember what he said. She knew noblemen and women did not share bedrooms, but...

She decided to just return to her room and await the bath and food. Her stomach rumbled, telling her that it couldn't arrive soon enough. As she stepped into her room, there was a knock at her door.

Hurrying over, she opened it to find a maid with a platter of food.

"Good morning, my lady. I've brought you some food." She placed it on the table where Colleen had eaten the day before. "Is there anything else you be needing, my lady?"

"No, thank you. This is fine."

The young maid curtsied and then left, closing the door behind her. Colleen settled herself in the chair and lifted off the domed lid. Coddled eggs, ham, sausage... There was too much food.

"Ahh, I thought I smelled food."

She almost dropped the lid at the sound of her husband's voice. Looking back over her shoulder, she bit back a sigh at the sight of him. Shaved, cleaned and dressed to impress. His britches fit him like a second skin, molding to his thighs.

He walked toward her, his stride confident. When he reached her side, he slid his arm around her waist and pulled her close. She drew in a deep breath, and her heart skipped a beat at the scent of his sandalwood soap, fresh on his skin. His lips brushed the top of her head.

"I want you to eat a good meal. You lost too much weight on the way here." He released her. "I have to take care of some estate business, and Mother is going to drag you around shopping."

When he paused, she looked up at him. His blue gaze roamed over her, and she fought the urge to straighten her hair.

"Don't let her bully you. If you are not up to it today, let her know."

She swallowed. "I-I think I'll do all right today."

He nodded, kissed her forehead and headed for the door. As he opened it, the footmen brought in a tub and the hot water for her bath. Once the tub was filled and she was alone, she stripped out of her clothes and stepped into the bath. Her body ached in unusual places, and she tried to ignore the memories of just how her body had gotten sore. As she washed, she thought of her husband. A confusing man. She knew he was a rogue, that he'd had many lovers. But he had also been so loving, so gentle last night. Even though he had been drinking. Women in the village did talk. And her sister had tried to tell her things, but thinking never to marry, Colleen had ignored her.

She sank further into the fragrant water, her musings focused on her husband and his personality. His actions the night before, so sweet, had touched her heart. She could accept that, but she could protect herself still. She would not fall in love. Ton marriages were not loving relationships. That took place outside of the marriage. That is why her mother and father had escaped their families, to marry for love. But that would not be her destiny. She and Sebastian were truly married now. There would be no annulment—and without a doubt—no divorce. She sighed. She needed to remember to keep her distance. Because she knew for a fact there was a good chance she could easily fall for the bounder.

CR CB CR

Sebastian arrived in the breakfast room just in time to be caught by Anna.

"Sebastian, what do you think you were doing running out last night? Poor Colleen was beside herself—"

"Anna," Sebastian chastised as he lifted the lid off the eggs, "I happen to know that until I came home, my wife was sleeping. And I wasn't carousing. I was at Daniel's."

"Hmmph."

"You were always witty first thing in the morning, Anna." He cut her a look as he glanced over the dasher filled with sausages. Her eyes had narrowed dangerously and not for the first time, he saw that his sister was an attractive woman.

He was still having problems dealing with the fact she was a woman. He sighed. This was going to be a vexing season with his sister on the marriage mart. Maybe Colleen would have some advice. Although she'd spent most of her life in the country, if not all of it, she might have some insight to the workings of Anna's mind. A smile pulled at his lips when he realized he had something to talk to Colleen about. And that could lead to all kinds of possibilities.

His sister cleared her throat, and he became conscious of the fact he'd been standing there mooning over his wife. From the look of speculation, she was dying to ask him what he had been thinking about.

Sebastian decided to change the subject. "Besides, I had to get the whole story of yours and Mother's adventures in finding me. Daniel has said he will have nothing to do with you."

She crossed her arms beneath her breasts and frowned. "I wouldn't care if he did." Her voice told him differently but he thought he would keep away from the strained relationship of his best friend and his sister. He set his plate at the head of the table and took his seat.

"Who is going to escort you to the Franklin Musicale Tuesday? I don't know if I will be able to do it, especially without Colleen. You know I can't appear at a social function without her."

"And rightly so, Sebastian," his mother said from the doorway. Neither his sister nor he had noticed that she stood there. "There is no reason to worry about that. Colleen will be ready to make an appearance. We will keep our attendance at a minimum since it has only been a few weeks since your cousin died."

The thought of Gilbert and Albert sobered him immediately. "Of course, Mother."

She smiled as she stepped into the room, taking her seat to his right. "No reason to get melancholy about it, Sebastian. Heaven knows how much I miss those two. And your aunt... Let's just say she could take Albert's passing, but when Gilbert was taken so soon afterward..." She sighed. "It was a terrible blow to her."

His aunt and uncle had been a love match, much like Sebastian's own parents. Both of them had doted on all their children, especially Gilbert who had been the eldest and the most genial. Sebastian knew she was probably devastated.

His mother took a sip of her chocolate, her eyes a little too bright for the subject, and he remembered the scene in his bedroom half an hour earlier. She cast a look toward Anna and seeing that she was preoccupied, leaned closer to him.

"I take it there will be no annulment." A strange mix of serious matron and humor colored her voice.

Heat rushed to his face and he felt his ears burning. It was ridiculous to blush in front of his mother. He was a grown man with wants and desires and a wife to keep happy. Sebastian knew the best way to deal with his mother was to be as pompous as he could. He straightened his spine and tried his damnedest to look down his nose at her.

"There was never any question of an annulment, Mother."

She smiled serenely. "You may not have thought so, but I have a feeling your wife might have wanted one."

He bit back a growl. Oh, how that rankled. Deep in his soul he was sure she was right. Colleen didn't want to be married, but he also knew it had nothing to do with him. He thought about his incoherent rumblings while he was sick and winced. Maybe it had a little to do with him, but it was marriage on a whole that she despised.

"That point is moot, as you well know." However, her belief that marriage was not for her didn't mean he couldn't convince her otherwise. Just thinking of the ways he would like to convince her sent a rush of blood from his head to his groin. He shifted in his seat to ease the pressure. His mother gave him a knowing look but said nothing as his sister sat next to her.

"I can't wait to get out today. It is going to be fun going shopping with Colleen." She sighed and launched into a detailed account of her plans for their shopping adventure. He almost felt sorry for Colleen...almost.

CQCBCQ

Colleen watched as the footmen carried the multitude of boxes up the staircase, still dumbfounded why one person would possibly need that many underthings. Granted, she was sadly lacking in that area with just two soft, white linen gowns, but her mother-in-law had refused to take no for an answer or to see the total for the bill. Colleen was positive as soon as Sebastian saw it, he would explode. Men didn't like paying for needless things. And no person needed six silk gowns for bed.

She sighed and massaged her temple.

"Colleen, I wish you would quit worrying about the expense. Sebastian isn't going to care one way or another."

She glanced at her mother-in-law who motioned to the drawing room. Colleen wearily walked down the hall as Victoria called out, "Fitzgerald, we'll take tea in the drawing room."

When they entered, Colleen immediately felt her muscles relax. Done in warm colors, the drawing room was perhaps more masculine in décor than one would expect, but it was inviting, as was the brilliant fire.

"Have a seat, my dear."

Colleen picked an overstuffed chair, settling back against the cushions, and sighed with pleasure this time. Victoria sat in the one opposite her.

"I love my daughter, but she does wear me out."

Colleen chuckled and then caught herself when she realized how rude that was. She looked to see her mother-in-law's reaction, but Victoria just smiled.

"That's okay, Colleen. Anna is an acquired taste. One of the reasons she scares most men away. Even with her dowry, and now being the sister to an earl, she requires a lot of energy. Much like her father that way."

She'd never heard anyone talk about Sebastian's father, especially Sebastian. Colleen had an idea that he'd died before Sebastian came of age. "So Sebastian isn't like his father?"

Victoria opened her mouth to answer, but the tea arrived, and it took a few moments for both of them to doctor their beverages. Once they were alone, Victoria seemed to sense Colleen's agitation at being interrupted, so she answered her questions.

"Sebastian, poor boy, is too much like me—always the thinker."

Colleen sputtered then choked on her tea. Victoria watched her with one eyebrow raised.

"You think Sebastian a simpleton?"

Colleen laughed. "No, not at all. But he doesn't always seem to think things through."

"Sebastian? I will give you some motherly advice if you don't mind."

Colleen nodded.

"Sebastian's problem is he thinks *too* much. He tries to look at things from all angles, figure out the puzzle."

"But that is a good thing."

Victoria smiled. "It can be, but in some cases, it can be bad. Action is needed at times. And Sebastian does have a pretty active imagination."

"Well, I can see where that might get him in trouble," Colleen murmured then flushed when her mother-in-law gave her a perceptive look. "What I mean... I..."

"Colleen, I was married and had two children, and in that way, I suspect Sebastian is much like his father. But in many ways, all men are the same. They don't like change even if it is what is best for them. Keep him off balance, do the unexpected. Sebastian may seem like an incorrigible rake, but he can be tamed. You just need to know how to handle him." The words made Colleen blush even more, so Victoria took pity on her and changed the subject. "Now, what can you tell me about your mother, your people? There is something so familiar about you."

Colleen shrugged. "I am not really sure about my extended family. Both of my parents came from titled families, but when they defied their parents to marry, they were both cut off. My father had money of his own, so they settled in York."

"What was your mother's first name?"

"Jane. I have no idea of her family. My father was, of course, a Macgregor and apparently far down the line for the title, but I gather he was a second or third son and was expected to make a good match. I know they met in London during my mother's second season."

For a second, a flash of recognition, something akin to a spark of knowledge, filled Victoria's eyes, but she masked it before Colleen could figure out what it was.

"It must be hard to be on your own."

Ah, just like her son. Change the subject when you gained your information and needed no more. "Yes. It was, but I had been handling our money for years, even after Harry moved in."

"Who the bloody hell is Harry?"

She started at the sound of Sebastian's voice, her teacup clattering against the saucer. Turning, she found him standing in the doorway and sighed. The man was too gorgeous for her well-being. The grim line of his lips did not dissipate the memory of how his mouth felt against her skin. She licked her own lips and watched the mischievous light in his eyes turn darker as he watched her tongue.

"Ho, Sebastian, you are losing control of your house and you haven't been back but a day."

It was then that Colleen noticed a gentleman standing next to Sebastian. Where Sebastian was darkly sensual, this man was a golden Adonis. He had light brown hair, cut impeccably, and calm topaz eyes. His clothes spoke of his station in society.

Her gaze drifted back to her husband, who was staring daggers at her. She glared back at him. One thing he needed to learn was that she would not be talked to in such a way. "Where are your manners?"

Stunned silence followed her question. His mouth hung open a moment before he snapped it shut. His eyes narrowed dangerously. *Oh my.* Her breath caught somewhere between her chest and her throat. Her heart beat hard against her breast. The man was even more gorgeous when he was mad at her.

"I told you Harry was my mother's second husband." Remembering her mother-in-law's advice, she did something Sebastian didn't expect. She stood and smiled. He blinked, his eyes losing a bit of their fierceness. That accomplished, she turned her attention to his companion. "I'm sorry for my husband's rudeness."

He returned her smile with enthusiasm. "After all these years, I am accustomed to it. Sebastian has always lacked manners."

Surprised by his ready flirtation, she laughed.

"That is quite enough of that." Sebastian stepped in front of his friend and walked to her side. From the look on his friend's face, the action surprised him also. "Colleen, this is my friend, Daniel, Earl of Bridgerton. Daniel, this is my wife, Colleen."

Daniel stepped forward, took her hand and bent over it. "It is wonderful to meet you, my lady."

He didn't kiss her hand, just the air above it as was custom. She could feel the heat of his breath on the back of her hand and her stomach flip-flopped. Colleen was not used to manners or interest from the opposite sex. Sebastian shifted next to her, and she looked up at him. His attention was focused on his friend, so Sebastian didn't see her reaction, thank goodness. Anger only made him more attractive, and for just an instant, staring up at him, she lost all thought. The scent of him, bayberry and clean male, surrounded her as the heat of him warmed her. And he hadn't even touched her.

Daniel released her hand. He looked over her shoulder and nodded. "Nice to see you in one piece, Lady Victoria. I pray that Lady Anna is doing well also."

Her mother-in-law moved into view. "Daniel, as I told you last month, Anna and I can handle things by ourselves."

"But now that Sebastian has returned, you will not have to worry about that." He turned his attention back to Colleen. "Sebastian and I were just discussing your marriage. I have a feeling you will take the ton by surprise."

His ready flirtation caused a blush to rise in her cheeks. Sebastian stepped closer to her. She started when his hand touched her waist in a possessive gesture. Colleen should have been irritated, but her body was already responding to the feel of his hand against her. She seemed to have no self-control where Sebastian was involved. His fingers stroked against her dress and suddenly, the memories of what he had done with those hands the night before filtered through her mind, tumbling over one another. She drew in a shaky breath and ordered her body to behave.

Sebastian's voice brought her back to reality. "Since I haven't announced it in the papers, I am sure it will surprise everyone, but I think we will have time for that before our first appearance."

"We will attend the Earl of Northrup's musicale. I had a note today from Lady Margaret, and she insisted that we attend. She knows we have returned."

Sebastian turned toward his mother. "She knows about my marriage?"

Victoria chuckled. "No, or she would not have been so insistent. She expects to throw her daughter at you."

"Good God, her daughter can't be more than sixteen."

"Seventeen and she just made her come out."

He sighed. "At least I am safe from her machinations." He looked to Daniel and smiled. "But Daniel here is eligible."

The color drained from Daniel's face. "Oh, no. Just because you are shackled..." He glanced at Colleen, color returning to his cheeks. She had to bite her lip to keep from laughing. "Sorry, no offense, but..."

She took pity on him. "I completely understand, my lord. Until recent events, I held the same view."

CR CB CR

Hours later, Colleen settled on her bed, exhausted. She thought she had recovered from her trip and subsequent illness, but shopping with her mother-in-law and sister-in-law would wear out the healthiest of people. Victoria, seeing Colleen's weariness, had ordered her to her room and sent her a tray for dinner.

Now, with her muscles relaxed, her body went limp, her mind shutting down. She removed her spectacles and set them on the bedside table. She sank deeper beneath the sheet. Sleep tugged at her, causing her eyes to drift shut. It was then she heard her bedroom door open.

Chapter Thirteen

Colleen froze. Her lungs seemed unable to function. A moment later, she realized it was the door connecting her bedchamber to Sebastian's. Her fear dissolved but her heartbeat sped up, her body warming.

He carried a taper as he walked around the foot of her bed to reach her side. She sat up, grabbed her spectacles and put them on. The shadows from the light bounced off the walls, and as he drew closer, the brightness grew. He set the candle on her bedside table and sat next to her on the bed. He was wearing his dressing gown and not much else, other than a seductive smile.

"No maidenly protestations?" Teasing laced his voice, so she really couldn't take much offense.

"It would be ridiculous, my lord, considering how I spent last night."

Even in the dim light she saw his eyes flare, his mouth curve. No matter the type of lighting, the man was gorgeous. The candle cast shadows against the curves of his cheeks and created the illusion of a loving, warm seduction. Her body reacted instantly. Heat gathered in her tummy and slid between her legs. Colleen didn't need to be told that this charmer was trouble. She was married to him. But she couldn't help her body's reaction. It probably was a genetic flaw on her part.

"I can remember exactly how you spent last night, my dear." His voice deepened and shivered down her spine. She suppressed the urge to sigh. Sebastian knew just what to say and how to say it.

"It is just...well...I thought the ton lived separate lives. That marriages—"

She stopped when he started laughing. "Woman, we haven't even had a honeymoon. There is usually at least a little time spent together at the beginning of the marriage."

She studied him, trying to puzzle him out. The man could probably have any woman in London. But he was here in her bed. Why? Then in a blinding instant, she had her reason.

"You want an heir." She didn't like the conclusion, but she wouldn't fool herself either. Colleen would rather deal in reality than fantasy. It might be boring, but she was rarely disappointed.

He frowned. "Not so much I want one, it is that I need one. But that is not the reason I am here."

She crossed her arms beneath her breasts, trying to quell the hope blooming in her heart. Charmers didn't stay around for long, and they definitely didn't fall in love with dowdy spinsters such as herself. "Really? So begetting an heir has nothing to do with why you are here?" She allowed caustic sarcasm to color her voice. She had to. Otherwise, the hurt of being used in such a way would show through.

"Well, that is part of it." His lips moved again, this time showing his dimple fully.

She didn't say anything because she was sure her voice would crack. Never had a man as beautiful as Sebastian flirted with her, let alone attempted to seduce her. It was mind-boggling.

He sighed and looked toward the window. She had no idea of what he was looking at since the drapes were closed and the room was dark. "Colleen, that has little to do with the fact that I have been thinking about getting back in bed with you all day."

His aggrieved tone made her smile as her head spun. He'd been thinking about doing *that*. A frisson of awareness flitted through her.

"All day?" Was that her voice? She'd never really heard that husky undertone in it before.

Slowly, he returned his attention to her. "Colleen, I have been thinking about getting you under me since the moment I opened my eyes this morning. And I assure you, not once have I thought about an heir, except the process of begetting one."

He placed a hand on each side of her hips and leaned forward. Again, the clean, musky scent of him surrounded her, and she had to fight not to lean closer to sniff. Before meeting Sebastian, she had never dreamed a man could smell so scrumptious.

"Colleen," he said, his face so close she could feel his heated breath across her cheek. "It is not easy to admit, and it is not easy to deal with, but I want you. I know you don't understand—"

"Oh, I do."

He drew in a deep breath and closed his eyes. "This would be a lot easier if you weren't so truthful."

Irritation crawled up her spine and she sat up straighter. "That is the most asinine thing I have ever heard you say, which is saying a lot considering the source. Not wanting me to be truthful, really. Do you want me to lie and tell you that last night was not wonderful?"

A burst of laughter rumbled out of his chest and he opened his eyes. "Only you would reprimand your husband when he is trying to seduce you."

Heat stole into her cheeks at the reminder of what was happening. She cleared her throat. "I never said I would be a conventional wife."

"Actually, what you said was that you didn't want to be my wife. You said you would tell people I died."

She couldn't believe he kept bringing that up. "You told me to say that."

He pressed even closer, his lips inches from hers. Her heart stopped for a beat and then seemed to triple in rhythm. Without breaking eye contact, he brushed his mouth against hers. Light, tantalizing, the touch of his lips against hers tempted, teased. He flicked his tongue against the seam of them. She closed her eyes and surrendered.

Never in her life would she have thought the mere touch of his lips against hers would send her emotions spiraling out of control. But the kiss heated quickly, her body reacting immediately. Her breasts swelled, her lungs seized. Desire and need ignited. When he pulled back, she tried to follow him. He chuckled and she opened her eyes. Before she could reprimand him once more, he was tugging at her spectacles, pulling them off, tossing them on the table, and then returning to kiss her.

This kiss was no longer the innocent brushing of his lips against hers. He took her face into his hands, deepening the kiss. Passion singed a path along her nerve endings as she slipped her hands up his arms to his shoulders and buried them in his hair. Her nipples tightened. As if sensing it, he rubbed his chest against them, and even through the layers of clothing, it was pleasure and pain all wrapped up in one. She couldn't seem to get enough of his body next to hers before he was pulling away again.

Confused, Colleen opened her eyes to see him getting to his feet beside the bed. Thinking that he was leaving, she opened her mouth to protest. Her breath came out in a rush as he tugged his nightshirt off. Even in the dim light and without her spectacles, she could see that he was beautifully naked. Every drop of moisture in her mouth evaporated as her gaze roved down his muscular chest. Yes, she had seen him practically naked in her cottage, but he had been half-conscious at the time. Now he stood before her, a golden god.

When her attention dipped from his chest to his abdomen and then farther, she panicked.

Good God.

He laughed. "I don't know whether to be embarrassed or proud of the expression on your face."

He climbed back on the bed but didn't cover her body with his. She looked at his face as he grabbed the bottom of her nightdress. Instead of pulling it off her as she suspected, he took it in his hands and slid it up her body, his palms brushing over her skin. A rush of tingles followed the same path. As he bared her, she didn't feel the cold air. All she could feel was the warmth of his hands, the heat of his gaze. She tried not to think of him seeing her completely naked, but it preoccupied her when the edge of the nightgown rose about her hips. She closed her eyes, trying to concentrate on the sensations he was causing. When he reached her breasts, his palms skimmed the sides, just the briefest of touches, and his thumbs grazed over her hardened nipples. She shivered.

A moment later she was laid bare for her husband to see. Colleen opened her eyes, but Sebastian never noticed. He kneeled between her outspread legs. As he stared down at her body, the look on his face erased all her doubts. Pure sensual hunger deepened the color of his eyes. At that moment, she didn't care if she was plain Colleen Macgregor from York who accidentally married an earl. All she cared about was that this man, her husband, wanted her. She wanted his skin against hers.

"Sebastian?"

He glanced up, smiling, but made no move to cover her. Instead, he brushed the backs of his fingers against one of her nipples. It tightened further, almost painfully. Again, her eyes slid closed as she allowed the sensation of his touch to seduce her body—her mind.

As he continued teasing that nipple, he leaned forward and took the other in his mouth. Relief filled her as she felt it close over her breast, but at the same time, frustration mounted. Liquid heat was now pouring through her, pushing her toward the pinnacle. Panic filled her chest, clogging her throat at the loss of control. It was true. She no longer held any control over her body. It was now Sebastian's to use as he wanted.

Colleen wanted to protest, to tell him she didn't like this feeling. At the same time, her body throbbed, clamored for his touch. Soon, he moved down her body, his lips brushing against her stomach, his tongue in her bellybutton, until he settled between her legs. She rose to her elbows, looking down at him. His head was level with her most private parts.

"*Sebastian.*"

He didn't even glance up. Instead, he kissed each thigh, his tongue sneaking out against her skin.

"Sebastian, I really—"

Her protest ended on a groan as he pressed his mouth against her. His tongue slipped between her folds. She gasped at the sensation as he applied himself to driving her out of her

163

mind. Within moments, her legs were shifting restlessly on the bed. Tension gathered in her muscles, curled into her stomach and then drifted lower. Frustration swept through her as her body tensed, and her mind tried to keep up with the need for release. He continued, his mouth moving over her sex. In the next instant, as if by magic, she exploded, her body convulsing, shattering into a million pieces.

Before she could recover, Sebastian was sliding up her body again. She slowly opened her eyes and looked up at him. Fierce and stark, his need was stamped on his face. Without so much as a word, he came into her with one swift thrust that had both of them sucking in their breath. He bent his head, his mouth taking hers in a brutally sensuous kiss. There was no seduction in this action. It was pure, simple, basic need. She could taste herself on his lips as he increased the rhythm of his thrusts.

Colleen moved with him, her body already gathering, racing, searching for another release. And in the next instant, she came apart again. Sebastian followed her a second later, shouting her name.

CR(3CR

Two mornings later, Colleen snuck into the library to search for a book to curl up with. All the fittings for her gowns were finished. Never one for fashion, she found the ordeal of shopping and fittings longer than she could almost bear. She prayed that the amount of clothing she had now would last her for the time being. She didn't relish repeating that experience anytime soon.

She shut the door behind her, making sure she didn't draw attention to herself. Leaning against the door, she closed her eyes and sighed. Her first true moment alone since she had recovered from the trip to London, and she was going to savor it. Before meeting Sebastian, she had lived a solitary life. She had a companion who had been with her during the daytime hours, but most of the time she kept her own council. Dealing with family and servants overwhelmed her every now and then. She just wasn't used to being around people from the moment she awakened until she slipped into bed.

Opening her eyes, she decided to find herself a senseless novel. She needed to immerse herself in a story and just enjoy. Perusing the titles, she ruled out any of the history books.

A sound caught her attention, someone sniffling. She turned to find Cicely, sitting in one of the chairs, her shoulders slumped over. Red eyes and nose, she didn't seem to notice Colleen. Since meeting the young woman, she had only seen her a couple of times. Each time, Cicely's mother, Prudence, had made some disparaging remark to her daughter. Watching her in her misery, Colleen realized just how alone the woman was.

"Cicely?"

She started, and her face flushed as red as her nose. "Oh, Lady Colleen." She jumped out the chair, several handkerchiefs falling from her lap onto the floor. "I didn't mean to bother you."

"You didn't bother me," Colleen said, smiling, trying not to let the young woman see the pity in her eyes. Pity was more embarrassing than getting caught crying. "And please, call me Colleen. I was plain Colleen Macgregor a month ago, and with everyone calling me a lady, it makes me a bit self-conscious."

Cicely nodded and returned the smile. Colleen noticed that Cicely was actually an attractive young woman. Not a diamond, that was for sure, but her face lit up with just that one little smile. Her hair was an indiscriminate shade of brown, but her eyes had flecks of gold. Being raised in society, Cicely had been expected to marry. It was her duty. With her quiet beauty and nervous ways—not to mention her overbearing mother—she didn't stand a chance of succeeding.

Cicely shifted her weight from one foot to the other and said, "Well, I will leave you—"

"Don't leave on my account. I am just looking for something to read. Can you suggest something?"

Cicely opened her mouth and then closed it. Taking a deep breath, she said, "I am not sure we would have the same tastes. I tend to like historical texts."

Colleen's smile widened. "But surely you have an idea of what is in the library. I was just thinking I wanted to escape for a little bit."

At that moment, Cicely really smiled, her whole face shining. "I do love to do that. I confess I sometimes indulge in a romance novel. It is nice to pretend to be someone else for awhile."

She hurried to the stacks and pulled out a book, handing it to Colleen. Leaning closer, she dropped her voice to a whisper, "This is my favorite. It is about a knight who saves his lady, although the lady is no shrinking flower."

Colleen glanced down at the title and noted she had not read it before. "Thank you, Cicely. I appreciate it."

She colored this time, in delight. "If you ever need help, let me know. You were right. I may not read all the subjects stocked in the library, but I spend a fair amount of my time in here."

Colleen nodded and watched as Cicely retrieved her handkerchiefs, smiled in her direction and left. Colleen settled into the chair Cicely had vacated, ready to read and thankful she didn't live the life of Cicely Ware.

CRCSCR

The next Tuesday brought her first appearance as Lady Colleen, the Countess of Penwyth. By midafternoon, her nerves were frayed and her temper sorely tested by her sister-in-law. She dearly loved Anna, but Victoria had been right. The girl required a large amount of energy focused on her. As she continued to prattle on about the upcoming event, Colleen's patience slipped away.

Anna, completely oblivious to Colleen's worries, didn't notice. "So when I told Ellen that you were going to attend tonight, she was beside herself. She could not wait to get away from me to tell others."

Colleen suspected the other woman just wanted to escape Anna, but she would never say that. She nodded as she tried to decide which dress to wear for the night. Both were laid out on her bed. Each of them was acceptable and much more beautiful than anything she had ever worn. The prospect of being watched like an abnormality didn't appeal. She wanted to present the best image she could. She knew their marriage would be questioned the moment anyone saw her with Sebastian.

Simply thinking her husband's name sent her pulse racing. If she had thought their marriage would be without intimacies, she was mistaken. But she didn't like the way her thoughts drifted to him at the oddest times, wishing he were there to share in some joke. Or the way each night, her body came alive beneath his touch.

As if conjured by her thoughts, her husband snuck up behind her and slipped his hands around her waist, resting his head upon her shoulder. She couldn't get used to the easy familiarity he claimed. She knew it was not normal for ton marriages, and it was something she hadn't expected in theirs. Apparently, Sebastian had no worries in that quarter.

"And what nefarious plans are being plotted here?" His breath tickled her earlobe.

Anna giggled. "Nothing worth mentioning. I was just telling Colleen how everyone is anxious to get a look at her."

She tensed, her stomach turning over at the prospect of the night's activities. As if sensing her tension, he massaged her back, causing her unease to melt away.

Ignoring his sister, he pulled away from Colleen, taking her hand in his and walking closer to the bed. He slanted her a look that told her he knew just what his sister was doing to her nerves.

"Trying to decide?" He nodded to the dresses.

"Yes."

He looked at her, then the gowns and then back to her. "Well, the grey is beautiful, but I really like the purple gown best. I think it would be amazing on you."

Giddiness welled up inside her but she fought it down. She did not need his approval. She was her own woman. When his gaze drifted down her body and then back up again, she decided that maybe she did a little. Perhaps pleasing her husband was not such a bad thing.

"So that decision made, I think you should lie down. Tonight will be a late night." His lips curved and her nipples tightened against the silk of her chemise. "A little later than usual."

His voice rolled over her, and the memories of their nights spent together in her bed and his flashed through her mind. She felt the blush creeping onto her face, but she was helpless to stop it. Her pulse raced and her thoughts turned deliciously decadent.

"Anna," he said to his sister, never taking his eyes off Colleen, "Mother said she needed to see you immediately."

"She did?" A mix of annoyance and distrust threaded his tone. "Why didn't you tell me?"

"You were talking too much. It made me lose my train of thought."

She muttered and shot her brother an exasperated look. Without another word, she left them alone, closing the door behind her.

"Did your mother really want to see her?"

He shook his head.

"Why did you lie?"

He grinned. "You needed to relax. Anna is best in small doses."

She laughed. "You are a horrible brother."

"Yes, but I am an excellent husband."

Arching one eyebrow, she waited.

"I know just what you need to relax." His voice had deepened, his eyes darkening. Her body warmed beneath his attention.

Liking his easy flirtation, she smiled. "A bath?"

He tugged on her hand until her breasts were pressed against his chest. "I think a proper lie-in with your husband would ease your nerves."

"Really? It's the middle of the day, my lord. Would that not be improper?"

His answer was to lift her off the floor, one arm beneath her knees, his other against her back. Excitement rolled through her, her body responding to the need he created within her.

"Sebastian?"

He strode to her bed.

"No. The gowns."

He muttered but turned and dashed to his room. Within moments she was beneath him, arching against him as he brought her to a glorious release. Later as they lay snuggled together, she watched him sleep and thought not for the first time that he was a dangerous man.

If she let him, he would steal her heart.

CRCBCR

"You have not accomplished your job."

He slumped his shoulders but said not a word.

"He has been home a week. Nothing has happened."

He could hear the fear lacing the steel tone. His employer was worse when worried.

"If the Earl of Penwyth died within days of returning with a new bride, and under suspicious circumstances, there would be questions. Maybe even an inquiry."

Cold grey eyes studied him. He felt the hatred that touched this one's soul. Hatred was a normal enough emotion but entwined with envy and evil, it could be deadly. Had been deadly.

"We cannot wait long. There could be a chance for an heir."

"It's only been a week!"

"I know she is sleeping in his bed. I told you he would not care. And worse, he seems to be completely bedazzled by her." The leather squeaked as his employer shifted in the chair.

"He hardly ever goes out."

"True. And I would like to avoid anything close to the house. They will be going out this evening. I am sure there will be a possibility there."

He wanted to disagree. But the ice in his employer's eyes stopped him. He would lose everything if he didn't do as commanded.

"If that is all?"

"Just make sure to include both of them. I do not want to think of any complications."

"You still will have to deal with his lordship."

Every muscle stilled as the air grew thick with tension. "I will deal with him myself when the time comes."

CRCBCR

"Any word from the runner?" Daniel asked.

Sebastian took his attention from his wife and glanced at him. They stood at the back of the hall, waiting for the music to commence. Society matrons, debutantes and the men they dragged to attend milled around the hall.

"No. Nothing yet. I don't want to dismiss his theories, or the fact that I was hit on the head and left for dead, but I have been in London for a week and nothing has happened."

Daniel chuckled. "You've barely left the house. Or I guess I should say bedroom."

Sebastian couldn't contain the grin that comment brought. "Well, I have been to the club a few times. And you know that I can't really go gallivanting around London with so much tragedy in the family and without my new wife. Colleen was nervous enough about tonight. Not to mention bringing the estates up to date."

"I don't know why. Your lady seems to have no trouble tonight. Who would have thought such a diamond would be buried beneath her ugly clothes and spectacles?"

Unable to help himself, Sebastian cast a look in her direction. She was chatting with his sister, their cousin Cicely and a few of his sister's friends. Daniel was right about the amethyst gown being the best one of the two. But that was only a small part of her appearance that had caught him by surprise.

In the last week, he had been privy to the wonders of his wife's body. She was tall, lean but curvy and more sensuous than he would have expected. He couldn't seem to keep his hands off her. Each night the anticipation of having her to himself, of stripping off her clothing, of taking her, left him with little blood in his brain. But now that he had witnessed this transformation, he didn't know how he would be expected to hold a conversation.

Her maid had fashioned her crimson locks in one of those styles that looked as if the tumble of curls would fall at any moment. A few locks had been artfully left down and every time she moved, they shimmered across her shoulders. She fit into the surroundings. He knew she had been worried about it, but she blossomed under the attention she'd received since they arrived. The color of the dress deepened the color of her eyes and made her skin look like fine ivory. When he saw the cut of the dress, her fine, delicate breasts laid bare for the world to see, he had almost protested.

The look his mother sent him told him he was not to say a word about the dress. He decided he would just have to look forward to peeling the gown from her body...

"Sebastian."

He started at Daniel's loud interruption. He looked at his friend and frowned at his knowing smile.

"What the bloody hell are you shouting for?"

"I said your name three times and you didn't respond. You were mooning over your wife."

Sebastian didn't miss the mocking tone in his friend's voice.

"I was not mooning over my wife. I was keeping track of her. There is a difference."

"So you were watching who she was talking to, making sure there wasn't a hint of impropriety?"

Sebastian nodded, pleased that he had diverted Daniel's attentions. Unease shifted through him, although he knew there was no sign of it on his face. He couldn't fight the urge to watch her, to think about her. It was driving him mad. Even when he had been young and still believed in love, Sebastian had never felt the ever-driving need to confirm the current object of his affections was near. It was almost an obsession.

"So you have no problem with the Duke of Ethingham sniffing around her skirts."

He whipped his head around and sure enough, there was Ethingham, moving in on the circle of people who surrounded Colleen. He was a known rake, garnering a reputation even worse than Sebastian's, and he had his sights set on Colleen.

Without another word, Sebastian strode in the direction of his wife and her admirers. He never took his gaze off Colleen as he passed acquaintances who tried to gain his attention. His mother introduced Cicely, Anna and Colleen to Ethingham. Just what was his mother thinking introducing all three young women to a known rake like Ethingham? He paused briefly to kiss over Cicely and Anna's hands and then dismissed them without another glance. Anger roiled through Sebastian when he witnessed the way Ethingham focused on Colleen, pausing to say something to which she responded with a laugh.

As he neared her side, Sebastian caught Ethingham's glance toward Colleen's cleavage and decided that he would have a talk with her when they returned. First subject on the list would be the necklines of her gowns.

The fine hairs on the back of Colleen's neck bristled the moment Sebastian stepped beside her. He touched the small of her back, just a whisper of contact, but she shivered nonetheless. It was getting worse. Just having him in the same room with her sent her senses on alert, but having him close, feeling his heat, inhaling his scent was enough to make a woman lose track of conversation and look like a fool. It didn't help that she could remember implicitly the delicious thrill that stole through her the moment he had seen her dressed for the evening.

She snuck a look from beneath her lashes at him. If she expected his attention, she would have been wrong. Instead he was looking—no glaring—in the direction of the Duke of Ethingham. Oh, this was not good. Sebastian's usually warm blue eyes turned colder as he studied the other man. Was this the man his wife had betrayed Sebastian with? He definitely was a rake in the first order. The way he had eyed her neckline had told her enough, surely. Sebastian could not imagine the duke would be interested in her, could he? She could barely keep up with Sebastian.

When she glanced at the duke to see how he was taking it, she was surprised to see the smile curving his lips.

"Ware...or I should say Penwyth. I was just talking to your lovely bride." The duke's voice no longer held any warmth.

"I noticed." Cold disdain dripped from the two words. No outright challenge, but there was enough of a threat in his tone to catch the attention of the people surrounding them.

She had to do something to diffuse the situation. "My lord, His Grace was just telling me about your days at Eton together."

For a moment, she feared Sebastian would ignore her or say something worse. Relief surged when he responded. "Yes, Ethingham and I attended Eton together. Although, he is a bit...younger than I."

Before the duke could respond, their hostess asked for their attention and proceeded to tell them the musicale was about to start.

"Ahh, I see we are to be seated. My lady." Sebastian nodded to a few acquaintances as he guided them to their seats in the last row.

Once seated, she leaned close to his ear. "Sebastian, I will not have you acting that way in public again."

Without turning his head, he said, "I apologize, Colleen, but know that Ethingham is not to be trusted. He has a deplorable reputation."

She swallowed the laughter that bubbled in her throat. "Really?"

"Yes."

Colleen was unable to stop a giggle from escaping. He looked down at her, his eyes narrowing.

"I am sorry, my lord, but you telling me another man has a horrible reputation is funny. I mean, I guess you would know."

His frown deepened. "Just remember, men in the ton are after the notoriety of whom they can seduce."

Her heart melted a bit at his warning. He was so attractive when he was serious. Misguided though he was, he was only trying to protect her. She patted his arm.

"No worries, my lord. I doubt he was interested in me that way. I have a feeling that the duke is more interested in beauty than brains."

He shifted in his chair and returned his attention to the stage, mumbling something under his breath.

"What?"

He leaned over, not looking at her again and said, "You are damned beautiful, and you know it."

Her breath caught, her blood pounding in her ears. The backs of her eyes burned. No one had ever told her she was beautiful, other than her parents. But Sebastian had said it as if it was an accepted fact. She knew she felt pretty tonight. The clothes, the jewels, the hairstyle... She felt transformed. But, in her heart she hadn't believed she truly looked much different.

From the instant they had arrived, Sebastian had focused on her. Despite the flirtation of more than one widow, he had attended her and avoided any other women. She couldn't remember ever feeling so special before. She studied his profile as he watched the musicians settle in their seats. Handsome, arrogant, difficult, seductive. And he thought her beautiful.

At that precise moment, Colleen stopped running and slipped headfirst into love.

CRCRCR

Douglas, Duke of Ethingham, continued to watch Penwyth and his new bride. He stood at the back of the room, not wanting to seat himself and get stuck at the end of the show. There was a certain widow he was planning on visiting later that evening. Matchmaking mamas were probably already planning how to corner him.

When he first approached the group, he'd thought to gain an introduction, do the pretty and then slip out the door. It was expected of him. As he neared the gathering, Lady Anna's voice had risen in excitement about some frippery she'd seen. He glanced at the mousy cousin, noting she avoided any type of eye contact with him. The moment his attention turned to Lady Colleen, something had nudged at his memory. There was something instantly familiar about her, although he knew they had never met.

"You are setting your standards too high, my friend."

He glanced to his left and saw that Bridgerton had joined him. Deceptively affable, the earl was Penwyth's constant companion, at least during the season.

As the musicians began a piece from Bach, he turned his attention back to the earl and his countess.

"Why would you say that?"

"I have a feeling that this is a love match."

Douglas had to agree. If it wasn't, from the smile the countess was bestowing upon Penwyth, the marriage was well on its way. He'd approached out of curiosity, knowing—as much of London did—that Sebastian claimed he would never marry again. After the man's first marriage, Douglas could see why. When he'd seen the spectacles, he'd been amused, but when he'd drawn closer, he'd been more than interested. He'd been charmed.

But when he looked down at her laughing up at him, he was struck by something familiar, something that slid down his spine, chilling him to the bone. He couldn't figure out what, but he would.

Bridgerton shifted next to him, and Douglas glanced at him. "Don't worry, old man. I have no designs on the countess."

The older man studied him for a moment, then nodded and casually walked away. Douglas returned his attention to the couple. Where had he seen her before, and why did he get the strange sensation that he knew her?

Chapter Fourteen

Colleen grimaced when she saw Prudence sitting on the chair in front of the fire in the parlor room. She'd avoided the woman for two weeks, since her debut into the ton. Although they shared a carriage to the events, Prudence showed her and everyone else that she wanted nothing to do with the new Lady Penwyth. Colleen was relieved Prudence had kept her distance. Not only did she think the woman a snob, but she was mean to her daughter. Constantly snapping at the young woman, Prudence was good at tearing down Cicely's self-confidence. Years of being criticized by her mother probably left Cicely with none. Each time she harped on the way Cicely dressed or the way she was always reading novels or attending history lectures, Colleen could see Cicely flinch. It was almost imperceptible, but it was there, and it made Colleen's heart ache.

Before she could turn around and sneak away, Prudence noticed her. Knowing there was no graceful way out of it, she entered, smiling at the frowning woman.

"I see that you are keeping yourself busy while your husband dallies all over town." The note of pity in the woman's voice angered Colleen. Since they had arrived, they had seen James exactly three times. Anna had whispered that James had a horrible reputation and kept a mistress.

"He is at Tattersall's today, looking for a new mare for me."

The woman pursed her lips, appearing as if she had sucked on a lemon. She stood, and not for the first time Colleen noticed how tiny the woman was. Her age did not show on her face, but the ugliness of her personality did.

Prudence approached her with small, mincing steps. When she finally stood in front of Colleen, she tilted her head up and somehow still found a way to look down her nose at Colleen. Cold and piercing, her eyes sent a wave of uneasiness shifting through Colleen.

"They have stories for their wives."

With that comment, she swept out of the room and hopefully out of Colleen's company for some time to come.

CRCBCR

A cool breeze whipped through the trees lining Curzon Street as Sebastian walked to his club. He could have taken his phaeton or gotten the coach out, but there were moments when a man needed time to think. For the past six weeks, his home had been overrun with matrons, all begging attendance with his wife. He scowled, ignoring the startled look from a couple of maids he passed. The dandies hadn't wasted any time either. They claimed to be there for his sister and Cicely, but they paid more attention to his wife.

His frown deepened as he stopped at the corner and allowed a few carriages to go by.

"Married less than two months and you already wear the face of a man run from his home."

Sebastian looked back over his shoulder at his friend. "If you had been there, you would have agreed."

Daniel smiled. "I just stopped by and was told you were heading this way on foot."

Sebastian studied a passing hack. "You saw what I was running from. You wouldn't have been able to take it, either. It would be so much better to just retire to the country."

Daniel chuckled. "I am sure you think so, and your wife might have thought so at one time, but that was before she took the ton by storm. Hell, even Lady Jersey likes her."

Silently, Sebastian agreed. While he hadn't wanted her to fail, he hadn't wanted her to be quite so...successful. Within days of their first appearance they'd been descended upon, and her appointment book had filled with meetings and outings. The only time he had her undivided attention was at night. Memories of the night before and this morning had him shifting his feet to ease the tightness in his trousers. And that unnerved him as nothing else did. He seemed to have lost all control of his reaction to her. Found himself wanting to spend more time with her, talking to her, just...being with her. He desired her, there was no doubt, but he also just wanted her attention.

He noticed the traffic had cleared and started across the street, Daniel by his side.

"What are you doing here?"

"I thought I would save you this afternoon. But I guess you saved yourself." Daniel paused then said, "Have you heard anything else from that runner?"

"Yes, we talked yesterday, but every lead has resulted in a dead end. James has airtight alibis for all three incidents. And maybe, just maybe, it was all a coincidence."

A flash of movement to his right caught his eye, and Sebastian realized that a carriage was heading toward them at breakneck speed. At first, every muscle, every thought froze. He pulled himself out of that state and pushed Daniel, who went flying forward to the ground, Sebastian jumping after him. He missed landing on Daniel by a few inches.

"Jesus, Sebastian. What the bloody hell was that?" Daniel said, struggling to sit up.

Sebastian's heart was lodged somewhere between his chest and throat. He swallowed and sat up slowly, knowing the fall would leave some heavy bruising. Looking down the street, he watched the departing carriage clatter around the corner. The buzz of conversation from onlookers swelled. "I think the theory that the incidents were a coincidence was just proven incorrect."

He glanced at Daniel and noticed the flush of anger on his cheeks. "Do you mean—?"

"I think we should summon Jenkins." Sebastian stood and offered his hand to help Daniel up.

As they surveyed their injuries, they discovered other than a few bruises here and there, they'd both escaped serious damage. The excitement over, the crowd began to thin.

"Thank goodness it is just a block back to your home."

Sebastian knew that showing up in this condition and then having a runner arrive at the house would tip off whoever was after him. Colleen would also know something was going on. The woman would decipher the root of the problem in no time. Soon she would ask questions he did not yet have answers to. She was too clever.

It chilled him to the bone to think of Colleen discovering what was going on. She might be somewhat helpful with that keen mind of hers, but knowing her, she would do something foolish. She might put herself in the path of trouble. Or...she might leave him. She hadn't wanted to marry him in the first place. With a killer on the loose, she might just abandon him. His chest tightened.

"We need to go to your home."

Daniel's eyebrows shot up to his hairline. "Why? Yours is closer."

"But it would raise suspicion, would it not?"

"If you are referring to the person who is attempting to kill all the Earls of Penwyth, I would say they will soon know you aren't dead," Daniel said dryly.

"Yes, but they would know I suspected something if a runner shows up at the house. We need to be discreet about this."

Comprehension lit Daniel's eyes and he nodded. "Right you are. Off to Bridgerton house then."

He turned to walk, and Sebastian stayed him with a hand to the forearm. "I don't know about you, old man, but I think we should hire a hack. My bones still ache from the fall, and a jaunt to your house probably won't help."

Sebastian didn't want to admit the other reason. At this point, he wanted off the streets. He didn't know where the next attack would come from, and his brains were too scrambled to pay attention.

CRCBCR

Colleen sighed as she looked out the window onto Curzon Street. It was midafternoon, and the ton were just beginning their house appointments, sharing tea, flirting. But today, the dreary grey skies, coupled with the north wind blowing through, had kept the crowds on the streets thin.

She knew she should be downstairs, awaiting the bevy of admirers and matrons, but she didn't have the strength at the moment. She'd awakened with a sour stomach and in an empty bed. Sebastian, she was told, decided to head out early this morning. Frowning, she left the window and walked to her vanity. A knock sounded at the door. "Come in."

Sally walked in and curtsied. Colleen fought the urge to look behind her and see what peer was in the room. She was still not accustomed to her new position.

"Begging your pardon, my lady, but Lady Victoria would like to know if you will be joining them in the drawing room soon."

It was on the tip of her tongue to yell "No!" and then run in the other direction. Knowing that would look a bit odd to the young woman standing in front of her, Colleen decided maybe that wasn't the best idea.

"Tell Lady Victoria that I will be down in a few moments."

Sally nodded and scurried out the door, closing it behind her. After checking her image in the mirror, Colleen shook off her melancholy and resolved to do her duty as the countess.

As she walked down the hall, she tried to push away the sense of unease that had held her in a stranglehold the last few days. At times, she felt as if someone was watching her, following her every movement. It could be all of the events she was required to attend. Sometimes, every now and then, she fought the urge to run away and hide. From everything. The people, the balls, the theater, it was almost too much. And then there was Sebastian. She hadn't been quite right for the last few weeks, knowing she was in love with a man who would probably never return her affection.

A flush of heat warmed her face as she remembered the night before. Sebastian had been very...demanding since their marriage, so she thought he might hold some kind of affection for her. But that affection stopped short of being love. It shamed her that she would take that, accept physical pleasure to be close to him.

A man who had been hurt as he had by his first wife would not fall in love so easily a second time. He had not spoken of his first marriage, other than the fever-induced ramblings in her cottage. Victoria had told her a few things, as had Anna, who had probably been too young at the time to realize just what was going on. Colleen didn't need an explanation for what went wrong. He'd given his precious love to this woman, and she had crushed it.

Since Sebastian and Colleen had returned to London, she'd cursed the woman an untold amount of times. What would it have been like to meet Sebastian unhurt, fully willing to give his love, share it with her? Colleen saw glimpses of that man. With his sister he was the typical older brother, teasing. Still, when she saw Anna and Sebastian together, she couldn't help but feel envy. And it shamed her to envy the love between a brother and sister. She'd never shared that with Deidre. Through the years, she had thought it was their difference in ages, her being almost five years older, and their personalities. But there was a greater age difference between Sebastian and Anna. Maybe she was just not the sort of person who inspired fondness.

Yes, her parents had seemed fond of her, but they were her parents. It was their duty. She fought back the rising tears. In the last week or so, she'd noticed her insane lack of decorum. For some unknown reason, she'd been a bit emotional and teared up at the most embarrassing moments. Colleen had decided the stress of her new station in life was causing her erratic emotions. That and being in love with a man who didn't return the feeling.

She had reached the top of the stairs that led to the first floor, not remembering most of the trip there. Straightening her spine, she took a deep breath. She did not want to socialize today, but she would do her duty. She owed it to Victoria and Anna for welcoming her as one of their own. And her friendship with Cicely, although still in the first stages, was something she had come to appreciate. And Sebastian...

The winding staircase was abandoned, and as she neared the bottom, the noise of the people gathered in the drawing room rose in volume. She fought down the rising nausea. She could do this. She *would* do this.

Strange, she thought, that there were no footman at the bottom as usual. Before she could register that fact, she felt a hand in the center of her back. Then, she was falling, almost flying through the air. She landed on her side on the thick Persian carpet. Sharp pain radiated from the side of her head as the light grew dim. There was a shadow off to her left. She opened her mouth and tried to raise her head to see who it was, to call for help. Her head throbbed and every bone in her body ached. The moment she moved, the nausea returned. She thought she heard someone calling her name, then her vision dimmed and she thought nothing at all.

CROSCR

Sebastian downed the brandy, some of the best that could be bought, and sighed with satisfaction. Before both he and Daniel had gone to clean up, Daniel had summoned Jenkins. After a quick washing, he borrowed some clothes from Daniel. They'd regrouped in his library.

Daniel swirled the amber liquid in his snifter. "Now, explain why you do not want to tell Colleen."

Sebastian sighed and looked over the rim of his glass at his best friend. He didn't know how to explain to him, his oldest friend in the world, the fierce protectiveness he felt for a woman he barely even knew. Daniel had watched the whole horrid incident with Elizabeth. He'd warned Sebastian not to rush into the marriage. He'd not liked Elizabeth, and she had returned the feeling. If he told Daniel now, Sebastian worried he'd get much the same speech about the foolishness of his actions. And explaining it might... Well, Sebastian didn't want to face that just yet. He didn't want to face the feelings that had been almost overwhelming him the last few weeks.

"I do not want her to worry. Her trip here has been so stressful, then the late nights and the galas. I'm not certain her strength has fully returned yet. Besides, she has grown very close to my mother and sister. I cannot be sure she wouldn't tell them."

"I think if you explain the situation, she would heed your wishes."

Daniel's defense of Colleen surprised him more than his own feelings of protectiveness. "But she is a woman, and women do tend to gossip."

He didn't expect the sharp bark of laughter from Daniel and winced when it bounced off the walls.

"You are talking about your wife, Colleen, correct?"

His irritation pushed the edge of anger. "Yes, you know I am."

"Colleen is probably one of the most levelheaded women—people—I know. I have a feeling if you went to her, explained the situation—"

"No."

"Just that?" Daniel shrugged. "Just no?"

Sebastian nodded curtly. He couldn't respond. Panic had joined the irritation, and they marched hand in hand causing him to take another swig of brandy. He didn't want to say what he was really thinking. Telling Colleen might be ideal. Unfortunately, Sebastian couldn't be sure the woman wouldn't abandon him because of the threat. Truthfully, he wouldn't blame her, but he didn't want to take that chance.

"No. That is final. She's my wife. It is my decision." When Daniel looked ready to argue, Sebastian turned their conversation in another direction. "What I can't figure out is, why like this? What is so important that they get the title now? They have had years to do this. Hell, my father has been dead for years, so the elimination could have been drawn out and not made to look so deliberate." He shook his head. "This is the act of someone who is very desperate."

The image of his uncle rose up like a rat from the gutter. Lazy, irritating and downright disgusting. It was well known that he kept mistresses and didn't try to hide that fact from his wife, Prudence. He was sure there was a case to be made that the woman drove his uncle to taking mistresses, but Sebastian still didn't agree with flaunting it in front of her.

"Your uncle is not the most likeable of characters."

He nodded, realizing that his friend was thinking much along the same lines as he was. "No, but there is one thing...he is lazy. He would never take time to plan something like this. He is not intelligent enough to come up with the plan. That is the strange thing. If he is the one behind it, someone else is there with him." It wasn't as if Sebastian had spent the last six weeks sitting around, but with so many dead ends, his frustration was mounting. "It could be him, or it could be someone else."

"You don't think he could do it?"

"Not by himself, no." But who? And why? The time line simply did not make sense to him. He shrugged. "I suppose it could be him."

"It would be hard to track every one of these damn cousins. You Wares are a prolific bunch."

Sebastian smiled. "There is that. I fear that my father was a disappointment to my grandfather."

"So it could be any of them, but I would gather someone at the top?"

Sebastian sobered. "Yes. I am lucky I was bashed on the head and left for dead. Otherwise, it would be my death they were investigating. I just don't see how they weren't going to draw attention to themselves this way."

"You are sure it isn't James? He would be the one who would gain the most."

"He doesn't need the money, or I would think not. Jenkins is making some inquiries. But all the sons were well taken care of. Grandfather believed in making certain all members of his family had money and land."

"So why isn't Cicely married? I would think she had a nice dowry."

Sebastian grimaced as the image of his younger cousin came to mind. Small boned, and a bit on the mousy side, she had quietly accepted Colleen as a cousin. The two women seemed to have formed a bond of some sort, both of them being bluestockings and Cicely on her way to being the spinster Colleen had been.

"She didn't take. She's been out for five years and has yet to have an offer that I know of. Pity, she is a nice sort of chit." He sighed. "Her mother is a detractor. Would you want her for a mother-in-law even if a fortune came attached?"

Daniel grinned. "I don't want any mother-in-law, but that is just me. However, I do see what you mean."

Sebastian didn't return the smile, knowing the life of a spinster with a mother like Prudence would not be pleasant by any standards. "As I said, she is a nice enough chit, but even I can tell she hates social occasions."

There was a knock at the door and Dobbins, Daniel's butler, announced Mr. Jenkins had requested a meeting with Sebastian.

"You have news?" Sebastian asked once Dobbins backed regally from the room.

The runner glanced at Daniel. "You can trust him."

He hesitated for only a moment to give Daniel a thorough study. "Well, my lord, I can't seem to shake this idea that your uncle is involved in this someway. So I have been tailing him. He has had some interesting chats with the Duke of Ethingham of late."

"Ethingham? What would he have to do with Uncle James?"

"Now, you see that was my question and what I wanted to ask you. Why would he meet with the man three times in two weeks? I'm not talking social occasions where they might accidentally bump into one another, either. And then there is His Grace's peculiar interest in your wife."

Sebastian forced his calm. "He has approached her on several occasions, true. But there is nothing to that. He tries to dally with many married women. I am not worried about Colleen."

"But did you know he has been sniffing around her background, looking for things?"

His blood ran hot at the idea that Ethingham had been courting his wife. What he had said was true. He knew Colleen would never stray from their marriage, but the idea of Ethingham investigating her background...

Sebastian's blood shifted and chilled. "You say the man has been checking into her background? Her heritage you mean?"

"Yes. The only thing I can think of is that your uncle might be trying to set the course for challenging your marriage."

He shared a glance with Daniel, but neither one of them said a thing. Still, the wily runner picked up on it. "There isn't a reason he could take to court, is there, my lord?"

"No." Daniel had taken care of the documents. "But why would Ethingham be involved?"

"It is said His Grace can get fixated on what he wants and won't give up until he succeeds. If your wife is what he wants—"

"He would be in a situation to take control of her life if I was out of the picture, and she was no longer the countess." He sighed. It seemed far-fetched, but he would have never guessed his uncle and cousin would be murdered for their title. "But couldn't they just be planning to kill Colleen as well?"

Even though it had been his words, they struck him to the core. His marriage to her had put her in danger.

"Yes, but unless they can arrange for an accident to take the two of you out, it would be even more suspicious. Discrediting her might be an easier way."

Daniel chimed in. "Think about it, Sebastian. If there is another death, and it involves Lady Colleen, it would be odd. Well, more than odd. And you know he can't take a chance with her being with child. That would make him lose any hope of claiming the earldom. Discrediting her claim would give him the earldom."

For a second, his mind wandered. All the talk of Colleen pregnant brought up the image of her swollen with his child. A sense of rightness swept through him. He shook it off when he noticed the two men were staring at him.

Clearing his throat, he said, "That might work, but I just don't see the connections. And why would he care about his daughter making a match? James cares of no one but himself."

"Unless he wants her out of his hair. He doesn't want to be saddled with Prudence and Cicely," Daniel offered.

"There is something else, my lord. Your uncle is done up."

That caught both his and Daniel's attention. "I thought you said he did all right."

The runner shifted his weight in the chair. "No. Your uncle likes the tables, he does. And he apparently has been losing a lot of money. His streaks have been bad."

Sebastian leaned forward. "Really?"

"There is even speculation that might be one of the reasons his daughter isn't married."

"You were right, Sebastian," Daniel said.

He sighed and rubbed his temple. "Is there anything else?"

"There is the unfortunate accident today," Jenkins said. "That was an act of desperation. Everything before has been plotted and planned. That makes me concerned. Your wife may be in danger."

"You said she wouldn't be. You said they were probably going to challenge her heritage."

Jenkins shifted again, apparently uneasy with confronting a peer of the realm. After a few moments, he sighed. "That may have been part of the original plan. But when an individual, a murderer, gets desperate, there is no telling what he or she might do. It is my duty to warn you."

The "she" caught Sebastian's attention. "Do you think this might be a woman?"

"Not really, my lord. There is no woman, save your cousin, who would benefit. And though I have seen some strange things happen in my time, I have never seen a woman of her character take charge like that."

Sebastian nodded. "I'll have to agree with you on that. Cicely is the type to faint at the slightest of things." He paused. "Poor Cicely. If James is at the tables, perhaps there is no dowry now. Her hopes are bleak indeed."

"I would suggest you take some measures, my lord."

"Measures?"

Jenkins' gaze grew penetrating. "I have a feeling you have not told your wife."

Sebastian ignored Daniel's chuckle. "How would you know that?"

He shrugged. "Most men think women do not need to know things like this. They think they can handle it. That they are protecting the women by not telling them. That might have been well and good in the beginning, but things have progressed, and although I think she was not the initial target, there is no telling what could happen."

"Colleen does not need to know. We know nothing for certain, and I will not have her all aflutter for conjecture. There is no threat to her life." And at that moment, he knew he could not stand not having her by his side. It was selfish and stupid, but desperation clawed at his stomach when he thought of her fleeing, running from him.

"My lord—"

The library door flung open and Gerry, one of Sebastian's footmen, rushed forward.

"I am so sorry, my lord, but this man insisted upon seeing you." Dobbins' voice rang of indignation and censure. "When I refused, he ignored me."

The sight of the tall, thin Dobbins trying to drag Gerry, who was built like an ox, out of the room brought a smile to Sebastian's lips.

"My lord, Lady Victoria bade me to find you," Gerry shouted.

"I will remove him in a moment, my lord." Dobbins tugged on Gerry's arm. He didn't budge.

Daniel laughed. "No worries, Dobbins."

"Gerry, what did my mother need? I can't see that it required you to follow me here."

"I went to your club, my lord, but when I did not find you there, I came here. I was there when my lord stopped by earlier looking for you."

"What," Sebastian said, trying not to get irritated with the young man, "did my mother want?"

"She wants you home."

Sebastian opened his mouth to argue but Gerry's next words stopped his comment.

"She says that you need to come home. Lady Penwyth, your Lady Colleen, has taken a tumble down the stairs."

Chapter Fifteen

"Colleen. Wake up."

Colleen ignored the summons. She didn't know who it was, but she wanted to be left alone. Every time she even thought of opening her eyes, shards of pain sliced through her head, radiating within her body. Unable to deal with it and the queasiness, her mind drifted back, enveloping her in peace.

"Colleen, I insist you wake up." Her mother-in-law's voice cut through the pleasant numbness. A sharp odor tickled her nose. She came awake with a start, the sunlight pouring through the windows, scorching her eyes. The nausea returned. She squeezed her eyes shut.

"Bright...sun." They were the only words she could formulate. And when had it gotten so bright? Why was she even thinking about that?

"Cicely, shut the drapes." Victoria again. "You can open your eyes now, Colleen."

It did feel darker. Slowly, testing the light in the room, she opened her eyes. Above her was the canopy of her bed. How did she end up in her bedroom?

She looked to her left, the area where she had heard her mother-in-law's voice float from and found Victoria leaning toward her. Struggling to sit up, she upset her stomach again. Worry etched Victoria's face, and she was so very pale.

"No, Colleen, you must lay down. The doctor should be here any minute."

"What happened?" Even to her own ears, her voice sounded weak.

"You took a tumble down the stairs. Not very far, thank God, just the last few steps. His Grace found you lying there."

Victoria nodded to Colleen's left. Although it took some effort, Colleen turned her head and it throbbed. Her body almost convulsed from the agony. The room wavered, but she fought the urge to slam her eyes shut again, determined to remain alert. When she completed the task, she was sure she wanted to die. She could not deal with the pain. But she focused her gaze on Ethingham.

She licked her lips. "Your Grace. Thank you so much for saving me."

His frown turned darker, his face no longer the vision of a carefree rake. "I did nothing to save you, my lady. I found you lying there at the base of the stairs."

"Still." She swallowed another wave of nausea. "I would thank you for your assistance."

"My Lady, Dr. Watkins is here." The voice was familiar, a footman, but Colleen didn't even want to try to think. Thinking hurt.

"Dr. Watkins. Please, come in." After a rustle of silk, her mother-in-law entered into her line of vision and spoke to a plump, rather jovial-looking man.

"My lady," Ethingham said, taking her hand. His blue grey eyes studied her, concern evident and overwhelming. "I will take my leave, but if you find yourself in a situation where you need help again, please, remember to call on me. At any time."

"Thank you, Your Grace."

After staring at her for a moment longer, he nodded and took his leave. She had the strangest sensation there was more to his comments than just a simple offer. The burning intensity in his eyes had struck her as determined. Determined for what, she had no idea, and at the moment she didn't care.

Victoria drew the older gentleman to the side of her bed. "Colleen, this is Dr. Watkins. He is going to take care of you."

"I'm fine, really."

Victoria shook her head. "No, darling, you need to have him examine you and make sure nothing else is wrong. Please."

Her fine blue eyes, so much like Sebastian's, showed her concern so Colleen relented. "Of course."

Victoria smiled, although it was probably an effort from the looks of it. "Cicely, let's leave Dr. Watkins to do his duty."

Sebastian's soft-spoken cousin had not said a word, but now Colleen remembered Victoria having her shut the drapes. Cicely walked up beside Victoria, her golden brown eyes huge.

"I do so hope you are all right, Colleen."

She smiled at the young woman. "I am sure Dr. Watkins will say everything will be okay with time in bed and a cup of tea."

Cicely nodded then turned, and Victoria followed her out the door.

"Now, young lady," Dr. Watkins said, smiling at her. "Tell me what happened."

CRCBCR

As Sebastian ran up the steps to his home, his heart continued to clench. From the moment Gerry had uttered the words about Colleen, terror unlike any he had known had taken hold of him and had yet to let go.

He rushed through the door. Before he could even ask Fitzgerald what had happened, he was confronted with a crying Anna. Her face, drenched with tears, sent another wave of fear rolling through him.

Oh, God.

"Sebastian." She flung herself into his arms, her body heaving with her sobs. "It is just so horrible."

He swallowed the panic rising in his throat and hugged her close to his body.

"Anna, darling, what happened? Is Colleen all right?"

"She fell down the stairs." She sobbed into his chest, clinging tighter.

"Anna, I need to know if Colleen..." He swallowed again. "I need to know if she is okay."

Her sobs grew louder. "There was so much blood."

Blood? "Anna, tell me." He tried to pull her off him, but his sister's hold was relentless.

"I daresay, Lady Penwyth will recover after some bed rest but the doctor is with her now."

Sebastian looked over his sister's head, his eyes narrowing on Ethingham. "Just what the bloody hell would you know about it?" Icy rage dripped from his words, and he didn't care. All he wanted to do was beat the man senseless.

Ethingham, holding his hat in one hand and a walking stick in the other, sauntered forward. "I am the one who found her lying at the bottom of the stairs and carried her to her room. The doctor is with her now."

"And you just so happened to find her? Tell me, Ethingham, what were you doing that you found her?"

"Sebastian, old man, no reason to get rude." Daniel's voice was gentle, especially for Daniel. Sebastian looked back over his shoulder at him and noted the caution in his friend's eyes. If Ethingham were involved in this, confronting him now would get them nowhere. Anger pulsed in his blood along with the need to smash something, someone. But he fought it back for fear of showing their hand.

He turned back to face the duke. "My apologies. Thank you for your assistance, Your Grace. I am in your debt."

Ethingham's eyes widened for a second, and Sebastian almost laughed at the comical expression on the other man's face.

He nodded toward Sebastian and walked past him. When he reached the door, he turned. "I would appreciate it if you would send word on Lady Penwyth's condition."

Sebastian wanted to refuse, wanted to tell the man to go to hell, but he needed to play it on the cool side. Make him think no one suspected his involvement. "It is the least I can do."

A strange look of confusion swept over the duke's features, but it was gone an instant later, making Sebastian wonder if it had ever been there in the first place. Without another word, Ethingham left. Anna still clung to Sebastian, but her sobbing dissolved into sniffles. With considerable effort, he pulled her from him and practically threw her at Daniel. Dismissing everyone and everything but Colleen, he took the stairs two at a time. When he reached the top, he ran down the hallway to Colleen's room. His mother stood outside, her face pale, her eyes red-rimmed.

"Mother?"

"Oh, Sebastian." For the second time in a matter of minutes, he had a female sobbing in his arms. "It is all so horrible."

The fear doubled. His mother was not a woman to dissolve into tears. "Mother..."

"Sebastian."

He turned his head toward Cicely.

"Colleen is just fine. The doctor is seeing her now, but it is just a bump on the head. There was a lot of blood." Cicely closed her eyes and drew in a deep breath. When she opened them again, Sebastian saw the worry, the pain. "But that is normal for head wounds."

Her rational explanation of Colleen's condition eased some of his fears. He pulled himself free of his mother. "I have to see her, Mother."

She nodded and Sebastian watched her rein in her emotions. He knew now she would be okay, so he dismissed all thoughts of her and without knocking, opened his wife's door.

The first thing he noticed was how dark the room was. Odd that a doctor would be doing an examination of a patient in a room as dark as a cellar. He looked over toward the bed and found Watkins packing up his instruments.

He glanced back over his shoulder at Sebastian and smiled. For the first time since he'd heard about Colleen's accident, Sebastian's stomach muscles loosened.

The doctor continued to smile as he approached.

"My lord." His voice was low and soft. "Lady Penwyth is just fine. The tumble down the stairs has left her with a bump on the head, a little loss of blood, but that is normal for this type of wound. Nothing dire in that. Everything is fine. She is resting, but I want you to make sure you keep an eye on her. I didn't give her anything for the pain. It isn't a good idea with head injuries. Wake her up every hour."

Sebastian nodded, swallowing the well of emotion clogging his throat. He couldn't decipher exactly what he was feeling. Relief most definitely, but there also was something so new, he couldn't figure it out, and at the moment he didn't care.

"She may get sick to her stomach, so make sure she eats light tonight."

After Watkins left, Sebastian moved toward her. She was so still, tiny even, laying there on her bed, her hair a mass of curls across the pillows. Pale, especially with the large bandage covering the side of her head. Sebastian wondered if everyone had been lying to him and she really was dead. Then her lashes fluttered and her eyes opened.

Relief poured through him, his heart finally dislodging from his throat.

"Sebastian."

He had to lean closer to hear her. She swallowed and her hand rose. He hurried to the edge of her bed, but sat down gently so as not to jostle her.

"Shhh, darling, everything is going to be all right." And he would make sure of it. "Watkins said you were okay. Everything is fine."

A tear trickled from the corner of her eye. He reached for it, capturing it on his finger. It was all he could do. Taking her into his arms, holding her close, would hurt her. But the need to touch her, to make sure she was here and safe was hard to fight.

"I know."

He hated to ask, but he knew he had to. "Colleen, do you know how you fell down the stairs?"

She licked her lips. "I don't remember much. I think I felt a hand against my back, and then I was falling."

Fury, pure and hot, crawled through him. His hands curled into fists as he thought of what could have happened to her because of him, because of their marriage.

"Watkins said everything will be fine."

She said it as if she could tell he was in a panic, and he really wasn't sure he was happy with that. A moment later, her eyes slid closed. He settled in a chair beside her bed, knowing deep down in his soul he would do anything to protect his lady. Even if it meant sending one of his own to the gallows.

CR CB CR

Douglas, the Duke of Ethingham, settled against the cushions on the carriage seat and tried to calm the rage boiling in his gut. Someone had tried to kill Lady Colleen. He knew it as sure as he knew his own name. He closed his eyes, trying to forget the bone-deep fear churning in his gut when he saw her laying there, her blood staining the carpet. Opening his eyes, he lifted his hand to his temple to rub away the headache and noticed it was shaking.

Nothing, save a whole bottle of brandy, would calm his nerves. The day's events drifted back into his mind, from the moment he found her until he left her in the doctor's care. At first, knowing there was something suspicious about her marriage to Penwyth, he thought the bastard might have tried to kill her. It had been hard to not seek him out and beat the bloody hell out of him. But then when he saw him, his sister sobbing in his arms and panic in his eyes, Douglas had known that unless the man was a world-class actor, there was no way he had anything to do with her fall.

The carriage drew to a halt in front of his townhouse. Coldness settled into him as he glanced up at the windows.

Thoughts of his childhood drifted by, his stern grandfather, his disapproving parents, the myriad of servants who had raised him. He shivered. He'd always wanted a house like the Penwyth's. A home full of warm, inviting people who wanted him there.

He sighed, knowing he was getting melancholy. Dwelling on his envy would not get him anywhere, would not help him keep Lady Penwyth safe. One of his footmen opened the carriage door, and Douglas descended, his thoughts turning to the accident. There had been callers around, Penwyth's mousy little cousin, his sister... Something was bothering him. Someone was missing. If he could figure that out, he would know who did it. And maybe then he could discover just why someone wanted the new Countess of Penwyth dead.

CRCSCR

Colleen sighed and gave her husband a stern look.

"Sebastian, it has been three days, and even Dr. Watkins said everything was fine. I can get up and move around on my own as long as I rest."

"Ah, but there is the thing I am worried about. You do not rest enough."

She bit back a growl and clenched her teeth. "I have been lying in this bed for three bloody days, and I want to get out of it. I want to take a bath, I want to sit in a chair to eat and I want to use the chamber pot without you, or anyone else for that matter, hovering over me."

His brow furrowed. "I have no idea what the problem is—"

Victoria's voice interrupted his argument. "Sebastian, leave the woman in peace for a few minutes. I am sure Colleen can make it to the chamber pot and back. You can take care of getting her bath brought up to her."

His lips turned down more and he crossed his arms over his chest. He looked like a little boy on the verge of a tantrum. He'd barely let her out of his sight for the past three days, at her side for every bout of nausea, every late-night chamber pot visit. And at times, she would find him looking at her strangely, a question in his eyes. But it would vanish as soon as he detected her regard. At first, she had been so overwhelmed with fear and pain, she welcomed the attention. Three days later, she was ready to throttle him.

"Sebastian, Colleen needs a few moments of privacy. You can return posthaste."

He hesitated, but then uncrossed his arms and bent forward. After a quick, hard kiss, he headed to the door.

"And don't even think of leaving this room without me." He tossed the ominous remark over his shoulder before shutting the door behind him.

"I know he is being a bit of a pain, but Ware men are a bit protective."

Colleen looked at her mother-in-law and realized that calling Sebastian any number of names would not go over well with his doting mother. Victoria chuckled. "Go ahead. There probably isn't a name I didn't call his father."

Heat crept into Colleen's face. "I didn't know I said that out loud."

Victoria approached the bed. "You didn't, but then I went through two deliveries with Fredrick and he was insane with worry. I believe with Anna they had to sedate him."

The wistful smile curving Victoria's lips made Colleen jealous. "It was a love match then."

Victoria smiled down at her. "Yes. I didn't want to love him, but he would just not go away. He was several years older than I, which is normally the way of it, and I wanted to have several seasons. Fredrick had other ideas." She sighed. "I will leave you so you can get a few moments without one of us Wares bothering you. Just...be indulgent with Sebastian. You scared him half to death. If you had seen him run up the stairs, you would understand."

With that, she left Colleen to her thoughts. After relieving herself, Colleen settled in a chair next to the fire, amazed at just how much effort it had taken to accomplish the simple task. The warmth of the fire relaxed her, and she allowed her mind to drift back to her mother-in-law's comments.

A small slice of hope slipped through her. Maybe Sebastian was coming to care for her. Maybe his ability to love had not been ruined by Elizabeth. The practical side of her warned her heart not to fall for him. Hoping for something unattainable would end up causing her more hurt in the end. But the impractical side of her, the one that longed for a marriage like her parents, like Sebastian's own parents, was winning the battle. She'd never thought to fall in love, but she had. And she wanted to build a relationship, to have a partner in her life, and she wanted it to be Sebastian.

Her hand stole to her abdomen. Dr. Watkins was not sure, but he suspected she might be pregnant. He'd told her the first few hours would tell if she had lost the baby, and since nothing had happened, he'd assured her the baby was fine. She was only a week late for her monthly, but she had always been on time. Now, she had to figure out just how to tell the father. She sighed. He would be even more protective of her if he thought she was carrying his heir. So until she was absolutely sure, she would wait, holding the secret close to her heart and hoping that it might come true. With that hope came the determination to win Sebastian's love.

She drifted to sleep, visions of tiny babies with dark hair and brilliant blue eyes filling her dreams.

‍CQCBCQ

Sebastian found her in exactly that position when he returned a few minutes later. Curled up in the chair, she looked so innocent, so young. The knot on the side of her head was now free of bandages and made her skin look even paler.

A knock sounded at the door, signaling the footman with her bath. After the men brought the tub and the buckets of steaming water in and left, Sebastian approached his wife. He hated to disturb her, but he knew she would be sore at him if she didn't get a bath. When he reached her side, he sank into a squat and stared. Two months ago he didn't know this woman, but at the moment he was hard-pressed to remember life without her. Just the thought of losing her sent a sliver of panic to his gut.

Reaching out, he brushed the backs of his fingers against her cheek. She stirred, leaning into his caress. A second later, her eyelids fluttered then she opened her eyes. The sleepy, contented look in their grey depths caused Sebastian's heart to skip a beat. Her lips curved into a smile as she rubbed her cheek against his fingers. A simple gesture, really, but that one movement sent a curl of warmth to his heart, and Sebastian was hit smack in the face with the fact he loved his wife. He loved Colleen. He waited for the panic to return, the utter and absolute terror of being in love. It had ripped him to shreds last time. Elizabeth had taken his love, torn it asunder and then trampled on it as she hopped from bed to bed. But this was different. This wasn't something that made him sick, that scared him into being a tongue-tied fool. It just felt...right.

"Sebastian? Is there anything wrong?"

He shook his head, still unable to find his voice. How had it happened? She was difficult, judgmental and downright sharp-tongued. But she was also honest to a fault, loyal and as beautiful on the inside as on the outside.

"Sebastian?"

"What, love?" His voice was whisper soft. He was fighting back the need to shout his revelations to her. Pledge his love and demand hers in return. He knew he had no right. She'd saved his life and then had her life completely disrupted. There was no way she loved him, or at least she didn't know it at the moment. He would make sure he spent the rest of their lives proving his love and earning hers. "Everything's fine. Your bath is ready."

He helped her to her feet. Sliding his arm around her waist, he pulled her body next to his. The feel of her soft curves against him sent a rush of heat racing through him. He bit back the urge to draw her into his arms, to make love to her until neither of them could think straight. Colleen was too weak for anything of the sort. When they reached the tub, he moved aside a bit to help her undress, but she stayed his hands.

"I can handle this myself, Sebastian." The embarrassment in her voice amused him. Since she was looking at her toes like they were the most interesting objects in the world, he felt safe smiling.

"Colleen, I have seen you naked before."

Her head shot up, her eyes wide behind the lenses of her spectacles. "I know that, Sebastian. It's just that...well..."

He chuckled, and she sighed, her irritation with him evident. "Well, it is different when it is just the two of us, and it is so much brighter now."

"How about I get naked also and then you won't feel alone?"

She colored even more, and he realized that teasing Colleen was really a lot of fun.

"No?" he asked, to which she shook her head. "Well, I am sorry, but you are stuck with me helping you."

Her shoulders fell in defeat. He finished undoing the sash on her robe, pulling it back from her body and allowing it to slide from shoulders to puddle on the floor. The chaste, white linen nightgown she wore was far from alluring. She had some very delectable silk confections he'd had the honor of slipping off of her, but even this made his body stand at attention.

Slowly, he undid the ribbon on the neckline and pulled the gown over her head, leaving her bare to him. Good God, she was a work of art. He wondered how he had ever thought her plain. She'd been covering up the body of a goddess, and now it was his. Her nipples pebbled against the chill in the room, and he licked his lips. It made him feel like an animal. Wanting her while she was weak and in no condition to make love. But there was something else, an underlying tenderness, a desire—a need—to show his love. Up until now, he'd only shown her that through lovemaking. His control was being sorely tested. He took her arm and steadied her as she stepped into the tub.

He sucked in a breath when he saw the bruises down the side of her torso. Purple and yellow marred her skin, and anger rolled through him again. She had not talked of the incident since that night. He had not pressured her, thinking that maybe the memories were too painful. If she knew who pushed her, she would have immediately given him their name. Both Daniel and Jenkins had insisted he ask her again, and he planned on it. Even though she said she had felt a hand at her back before she fell, she would not discuss the prospect that she might have been pushed. Every time he tried to discuss it, she would get upset and truthfully, she could not help him. There was no way for her to know who might have pushed her. Since there had been no witnesses, Sebastian was certain even with Jenkins poking around, they would come up empty. Again.

She sank into the water and Sebastian settled into a chair near the tub, trying to ignore the sound of her splashing. He shifted on his chair and concentrated on counting backwards from one hundred. Her contented sigh had him losing count.

"Sebastian?" Her voice had deepened in pleasure with her bath.

He gritted his teeth. "Yes, love?"

A little more splashing, and he shifted again, his body throbbing with desire.

"Is there any reason why you couldn't join me in the tub?"

Chapter Sixteen

Sebastian didn't know if he'd heard Colleen correctly at first. His head whipped around and stared at the back of hers. Her hair was a mass of curls piled on top of her head, a few wisps escaping and laid against her neck. Lord, he wanted to press his lips right there, taste her skin.

Convinced all the blood had drained rational thought from his brain, he hesitated and then asked, "What?"

Oh, brilliant. He sounded like a fool.

She chuckled, the sound of it spiraling through him, warming him. He realized he had begun to live for her happiness. Every time she showed it, he felt as if he owned the world.

"I asked if you wanted to join me. There is plenty of room, Sebastian."

The teasing in her voice was almost his undoing. Not once since their first night together had she initiated their lovemaking. He swallowed and curled his fingers into his palms.

"You are still recovering." He sounded like a bloody prig, but he refused to take advantage of her. She had been through an ordeal, and the last three days he'd watched her struggle through the pain.

"I saw Dr. Watkins this morning. He said I was fit."

God, he wanted her. He wanted to pull her out of the bath, throw her on the bed and plunge into her. He nearly shook with the need.

"He said that you still needed rest."

She tsked. "He said not to overdo it. There is a difference, Sebastian." Even her chiding tone turned him on. He was going out of his bloody mind with want, and the woman was pushing him, prodding him, driving him half-mad with desire.

"Colleen, you need rest to heal properly." He bit the words out between his teeth.

She sighed. "If you don't want to, Sebastian, then just say so." She shrugged and continued washing herself as if she hadn't just asked him to join her to frolic in the tub.

Not want her? He was about to go crazy from refusing the need to touch her. This was a test of his character. He knew it. Someday, God would pay him back because he resisted her.

"It isn't that I don't want you, Colleen." Even to his own ears his voice was rougher, deeper, needy.

She paused and then returned to soaping her arms. "Really? You have an odd way of showing that you do want me."

Was she that obtuse? He rose to his feet and walked to the side of the tub. He looked down at her as she leaned back to meet his gaze. The steam from the bath had fogged her lenses a bit. With her tousled curls and her earnest expression, she looked like a scolding nanny; a very sexy and somewhat debauched nanny. And she was his to do with as he pleased. He smiled and dropped to his knees beside the tub. Skimming his fingers along the surface of the water, he watched her smile in triumph. But he wasn't letting her off that easy. She'd known he wanted her and had teased him. Now it was time to pay her back.

Cocking her head in a completely coy fashion, she asked, "So are you going to join me in the tub?"

She shifted, causing the water to slosh against the side. Once the waves subsided, her nipples peaked above the water. She drew in a sharp breath as he skimmed his fingers over the turgid tips.

"I would like that very much."

He watched in delight as the depths of her grey eyes darkened in arousal. She licked her lips and then moaned when he tweaked one nipple.

"Sebastian."

His name was a heated whisper. Her eyelids slid closed, but not before he saw her arousal flare higher. The scent of vanilla and cinnamon surrounded him. Had he ever known a woman he wanted to devour like he did his wife? Innocent and wanton. So strong, yet so vulnerable. A mass of contradictions that left him confused but also intrigued. Desire hummed through him. He wanted to join her in the bath and love her slowly, but he knew that would not happen tonight. Being careful of her bruising, he slipped his hands beneath her arms and pulled her out of the tub. Water sloshed, wetting his clothes and the carpet, but he didn't care. Colleen's mouth opened to protest.

He didn't give her a chance. The moment he had her clear of the tub, he pulled her against him, his mouth devouring hers.

Had he ever tasted anything as sweet as this? No woman could tempt him the way she could. He'd had mistresses who had been trained in the art of seduction, and not one of them had been able to bring him to quiver with lust in such a manner. It had to do with her openness. Never did he wonder of her attention, it was never feigned. Each time he touched her, she gave herself to him in joy.

She wrapped her legs around his waist, her hands threading through his hair. She moaned as his tongue slipped past her lips, into her mouth, tasting the sheer joy that was Colleen. He held her against him, his hands on her rear end, and walked to the bed. He did not break the kiss but did open one eye so as not to cause them serious injury by tumbling to the floor and landing on top of her.

He made it to the bed amazingly enough and lowered her onto it. Pulling away with considerable effort—the woman didn't want to stop—he clawed at his trousers. When he undid the last of the buttons he sighed, relieved the pressure was finally gone.

Standing in the vee of her legs which were dangling off the bed, he moved closer to her. Before he could cover her body with his, Colleen sat up, her eyes wide with wonder behind her lenses. He reached for them, but she batted his hands away. Without any artifice, she studied his member. She trailed a finger down the length of it and then back. Just a simple touch, but watching her hand on his cock, witnessing her joy of discovery, was probably one of the most erotic things he'd ever seen in his life. When she wrapped her hand around him, he sucked in a breath and she immediately released him.

"No."

He grabbed her hand and placed it on him, showing her just what he liked. As she moved her hand, he dipped his head back, closed his eyes and enjoyed the feel of her skin next to his. Before long, her strokes became more than he could stand. He removed her hand from his cock and pushed her back on the bed. After stripping off his trousers, he covered her body with his. True to form, she started to protest. He stopped her with a wet, open-mouth kiss that ended with her moaning.

She planted her feet on the bed and pushed herself against him. The very heat of her core warmed his cock. At the moment, her mouth on his, their skin slick and hot, Sebastian almost lost control. He understood, even if she did not, that this was no longer about lust or animal instinct, but his love for her.

As she moved against him, he let her guide their rhythm, their lovemaking. His body clamored for release, for the need to sink inside her warmth, but he held back. As she pressed harder, he knew he would go insane if he didn't gain some relief soon. He grabbed her hips and rolled them over, reversing their positions.

Colleen sat up, her confused frown pulling a laugh from him.

"Sebastian?"

Uncertainty and arousal colored her voice. Sebastian thought it was the most beautiful sound in the world.

"Take me inside you, Colleen."

Her eyes rounded and then dilated with pleasure. She lifted off of him, taking his member into her hand and slowly sinking down on him. She didn't take all of him in. Keeping her strokes shallow and the rhythm slow, Colleen drove him mad. Sliding his hands up her thighs, he gritted his teeth, determined to allow her to set the pace.

Soon, her movements increased in speed. He felt her slickness intensify as she raced closer to the pinnacle. He moved his hands to her breasts and watched in delight as her head dropped back and she moaned his name. Her strokes became frantic, and he knew with one touch he could send her over. Sliding his hand to her sex, he pressed against the hardened nub. A moment later, she screamed his name, her body convulsing with her release. He could wait no longer. Grabbing her hips, he pushed himself into her to the hilt. A few strokes and he joined her, her name on his lips.

She collapsed on top of him, and for a few minutes, he lay contented. Nothing had ever felt as good as his wife, her head against his shoulder, her breath a whisper on his skin.

Knowing the position would not be conducive to sleep, he pulled her from on top of him with regret. After settling her against the pillows, he extinguished the candles, climbed beside her in bed and gently removed her glasses.

As if by instinct, she rolled into his arms and snuggled against him. He gathered her closer and allowed the newfound feeling of love to fill him, warm him from the inside. He kissed the top of her head and smiled when she emitted an unladylike snore telling him she was already asleep.

Feeling secure she would not hear him, he kissed her head and said, "I love you, Colleen."

CRCGCR

Hours later Colleen awoke to a darkened room. Sebastian shifted next to her, his body warm, his arms wrapped around her waist. Slowly, so as not to disturb her husband, she reached to her nightstand, found her glasses and donned them. She settled back against his side, his arm winding around her waist again, his hand resting on her backside. A sense of well-being, of belonging, swept through her. There was something so right about lying beside Sebastian, the sound of rain against the window, her body full of sleepy contentment.

She had thought Sebastian had shown her the depths of his sensuality since their first night together, but tonight had been a different experience altogether. Something lurked there, beneath the surface of her complex husband, that she had felt whisper across her soul. Colleen didn't know if she should be happy or scared or both.

215

"That is not a look a man dreams of seeing on the face of the woman he just made love to scant hours before."

She looked up at him and her breath caught. Heavy-lidded eyes, lips curled into a seductive smile, he was the picture of contented male beast. He reminded her of a leopard who was satisfied with one meal, but never taking his mind off his next snack. She shivered as warmth stole through her, her nipples tightening.

"I was just thinking."

"Another thing a man does not dream of hearing from his lady love." He pulled her on top of him. She wiggled against him, delighted that she felt his member growing hard against her sex. He swatted her derrière. "Stop that. I can't concentrate."

She bent her head and kissed his chest, swiping her tongue against his skin.

"Colleen, stop it."

He sounded so stern. The thought of Sebastian Ware, rake of the first order, admonishing her for trying to be seductive made her laugh.

"Very funny especially when you are not the one in pain," Sebastian said.

Worried, she pulled her head up, smacking him squarely on the chin.

"You're in pain?" She didn't want Sebastian to ever be in pain.

He rubbed his chin as he studied her. "Yes, but it is a good kind."

She frowned. "There is a good kind?"

He massaged her backside. "You know how it feels right before you explode while we are making love?" She nodded, not being able to utter a word. His hand against the tender skin on her rear end was making it hard to concentrate. "It is that kind of pain."

Satisfied, she snuggled closer and sighed.

"Colleen, I need to ask you...have you remembered anything from the day you fell?"

She closed her eyes, trying to remember, trying to grasp the one thing that would help. "No, Sebastian. I have tried, believe me, but I can't remember anything except feeling something on my back and then falling. The next thing I remember I was here in this bed, your mother hovering over me. And His Grace."

Sebastian muttered something she couldn't quite decipher. She sat up fully, ignoring the sheet as it fell around her hips. A frown pulled at his lips as he looked up at her.

"Sebastian, is there something I should know? Something you know about him?"

A look came and went in his eyes, an emotion she could not figure out. It was gone so fast she thought maybe she had imagined it.

"No, Colleen. I just don't like the way he looks at you. He is known for his many conquests."

She crossed her arms beneath her breasts and tried to ignore the flare of desire in his eyes. "Sebastian, I have no idea why you are worrying about him. I am not attracted to him in the least. And why would I be a conquest he would want? Good Lord, the man is a duke. I have seen the number of eligible and not-so-eligible women line up when he enters a room. Why on earth, with all that beauty beating down his door, would he want me?"

His frown deepened. "Colleen, first of all, I have told you time and time again that you are bloody beautiful. Not one of those women can compare to you. And secondly, you are an

217

intriguing woman. You are considered an Original by the ton. Beauty and brains. Not that easy to find." He blew out a disgusted breath. He was the picture of an aggravated male. Her heart melted at the sight. Was there any way she could not love this man? "Not beautiful? The woman thinks herself plain? Answer me this, if you are so plain why do I ache with wanting you? I can't think for wanting you, and when I am away from you it is worse."

As if he could no longer stand it, he grabbed her arms, pulling her face to his. Taking her mouth in a rough kiss, he rolled over, reversing their positions. By the time he finished kissing her, her head was spinning, her body aching, needing his touch.

"If you don't believe me, I will just have to prove it to you," he said, kissing his way down her body. His tongue flicked over her skin with each kiss, her body already heating with anticipation.

He settled between her legs. After brushing a kiss to the sensitive skin on the inside of her thighs, he pressed his mouth against her sex. All thought dissolved, other than the fact that this man was touching her, loving her. Moments later, she was moaning his name, and he was traveling up her body. He entered her, one thrust to the hilt, and went about building her desire again. When she thought she would be out of her mind if she didn't find some release, she exploded, her body convulsing beneath his as he thrust once more and joined her in bliss.

CR CB CR

"Why did you do it?" Jasper asked in irritation. "I thought it would be months before we had to take care of the woman."

Disgust curled in his stomach, upsetting the contents. He swallowed, trying to keep the bile from rising to his throat. Jasper had never killed a woman, never even thought of it. His mother would be so very ashamed of him. And then there were the feelings. Someone was always watching him; he knew that.

His employer stared at him with cold eyes. "She is breeding. I had to do something. You have waited so long, they may have created an heir."

"Breeding? They have been married for less than two months. And how do you know if she is breeding? Has there been an announcement?"

His employer laughed. "Apparently you are not acquainted with my nephew. Knowing him, they have been rutting since the moment the vows were said. Besides that, I have quizzed the upstairs maid. She has not had one monthly since they returned."

Another wave of nausea swept over him and heat stole across his cheeks. He had never known anyone who was so plain speaking, especially a peer. Sweat popped out on his forehead.

"I thought you said there was something with the marriage, that somehow you could prove it was not legitimate."

The sigh was filled with irritation. "Yes, there was a chance, but he returned and no doubt had Bridgerton do something about it. No matter, it is now legitimate in the eyes of the law."

"You could wait until she has the child."

"Wait until she has the child, to see if I have lost all?"

Jasper hesitated then nodded. His employer scoffed. "That is a brilliant idea. And just what do I do if it is a boy? If there is an heir? Do we wait until he gets old enough so it won't be too scary for you to kill him? You couldn't kill a woman without stuttering. What are you going to do when it is a precious little boy?"

Something cold, colder than Jasper had ever felt, slithered through him. His employer's ranting had grown more rampant, more...delusional over the months. Jasper rose from his chair.

"Let me know when you need me next, and I will do what you want."

The laughter was there again, calculated and hysterical. The laughter of a person gone mad. Icy fingers trailed down his spine.

"What I want? What I want is someone who knows what the bloody hell they are doing."

A second later, his body shivered with understanding as his employer took out a gun, leveling it at his heart. Jasper reacted as quickly as his mind could, frozen with fear as it was, and turned to run out the door. The report of the gun sounded and the smell of powder filled the air as he felt the bullet smash into his back. A burst of burning pain squeezed his heart then spread through his body as he fell to the floor.

The last thought as his blood pulsed out of him, drawing him further into the darkness, was of his mother and how very ashamed she would have been of him.

Chapter Seventeen

For the next week, Colleen held the secret of her pregnancy close to heart. There were so many moments when it was difficult, such as now when she wanted to blurt it out to Sebastian, but she held her tongue. She had not wanted to raise his hopes.

"That is a serious look for a woman taking a bath with her husband."

She glanced up at him. Shadows of the candlelight flickered over his skin. Since her suggestion the week before, Sebastian had insisted on several baths with her. They spent more time exploring their desires than they had washing, she thought with a sigh. She could still remember blushing when trying to explain to the housekeeper, Mrs. Nettles, why there was so much water on the floor.

"It's nothing, just thinking about tomorrow night. Do we have to go?"

He took her hand in his, raising it to his mouth. His eyes never leaving hers, he kissed each finger.

"If you do not want to, we do not have to go. But you will have to make a ball appearance at some time, Colleen. It is better to get the wretched thing over with so you can quiet your nerves."

She pulled at her bottom lip with her teeth, then settled against him again, her back to his chest. "Am I that transparent?"

He chuckled, the sound of it vibrating against her back. "Only to me, love. You know how to dance, you have proven that. Did your mother teach you?"

It was the first time he had asked her about her mother or her upbringing. A spurt of joy filled her heart.

"Yes. Both she and my father loved to dance. They would clear the parlor and Deidre would play the piano. They knew all the latest dances even though it had been years since they met in London."

"Do you know anything about your mother's family?"

She shook her head. "No. I know we are part of the Macgregor Clan because of our surname, but my mother never spoke of her family. I think it was too painful for her. From what I gather, her father all but disowned her when she ran off with my father."

"Was your father much of a rake?" She could hear the smile in his voice and smiled in reaction.

"No. Well, he might have been, but as a young girl I didn't think of him as anything more than my father. Mother's father objected on the grounds Father was a third son, not much money." She frowned. "No, I don't even know that. Father had a lot of money, and I know it wasn't just from the land surrounding the cottage."

Sebastian was silent for a moment, then said, "Were you very lonely after your father's death?"

The memory of the time after her father's death stole into her vision. Sadness swept over her again, dampening her joy of sharing her bath. "At first, it was not too bad. There was still Deidre, Mother and I, and we had enough money not to worry.

222

Then my mother met Harry Philpot, local charmer and all-around drunkard."

He didn't say anything for a few seconds. "Did he...did he ever hurt you?"

She knew the question had been hard for Sebastian. The subject matter notwithstanding, he didn't want to ask, but to demand. "No. He was a drunk, but not an overly violent drunk, just...not pleasant. What drunk is?" She shrugged. "The worst part was seeing my mother slowly die and he not care. Then Deidre left when she turned seventeen. A year later, she returned pregnant and was dead a few months after that. Harry froze to death that very year, after falling in a ditch in the snow."

His arms slid around her, hugging her close to him, kissing her temple. "I am so sorry, Colleen."

Unbidden, tears rose in her eyes, but she blinked them away. Anyone else, she would have suspected they pitied her. But Sebastian's voice was so tender, so loving, she couldn't fight the expectation growing within her. She knew without a doubt, he truly cared for her, and someday, sometime in the future, maybe he could bring himself to love her.

And then maybe he would tell her about the pain shadowing his own heart.

CRCSCR

Sebastian watched his wife sleep with a new sense of wonder. She'd been left alone very young. From the time her father died, she had been virtually on her own, with a mother who had not been able to function without a man by her side, and a sister who ran when she had the first chance. She had shouldered the responsibility and persevered.

He pulled her close and she sighed, borrowing her head beneath his chin. Sebastian and Daniel had met with Jenkins again, discussing possible plots. There seemed to be no earthly reason why Ethingham would have tried to kill Colleen. If Ethingham had approached her, Colleen would have told him. He knew that deep down in his soul.

Frustrated that he couldn't find one thing, one bloody clue, Sebastian had ranted to Daniel about retiring to the country. It had seemed a good idea until Daniel said that if it were a member of the household, it might make it easier to create an "accident" with miles of land around the Penwyth estate.

Sighing, he hugged Colleen. He didn't like taking her out tomorrow night, but his mother was growing suspicious, as was the ton, on why he wouldn't attend balls with his wife. He couldn't very well tell his mother someone wanted him dead and Colleen out of the picture by any means possible. Daniel would be there, and they had eyes among the servants at Denham's house, set in place by Jenkins. There would be no way in hell anyone would harm Colleen, he couldn't let it happen.

Sebastian didn't think he could stand to have her ripped away from him, now that he had found his heart.

CRC3CR

"My lady?"

Colleen looked up from the book she was reading to find Sally staring at her. She smiled and the girl flushed. Since her accident, Sally had blamed herself for not waiting to attend Colleen down the stairs. No matter how many times Colleen had reassured her that it was not her fault, Sally seemed unable to forgive herself.

"The Duke of Ethingham is here to see you."

Oh, this was not good. She didn't know what to do. Sebastian was out on an errand and Cicely, Anna and Victoria had all gone out on a shopping expedition. Colleen knew there was probably a way to refuse him, but he was a duke.

"Thank you, Sally. Please tell His Grace I will see him here and make sure to arrange for some tea to be brought in."

Sally hesitated then bobbed a curtsy. A moment later she returned with Ethingham.

Colleen rose as he entered and noticed that when Sally departed, she left the door open.

"Your Grace, it is so nice to see you again."

He smiled a predatory smile, but Colleen knew that Sebastian was wrong. Just like her husband, seduction was probably second nature to Ethingham, and his every reaction was built for that. He bent over her hand, kissing above the skin.

"It is nice to see you looking so well, Lady Penwyth."

"Won't you have a seat?"

He nodded but waited for her to seat herself again. Once he settled, there were a few moments of awkward silence.

She cleared her throat. "Might I ask you the nature of your visit?"

He flushed, just a simple staining of red across his sculpted cheeks, and Colleen panicked. Had Sebastian been right about the duke?

"My Lady Penwyth—"

Before he could speak, one of the parlor maids interrupted him. Once the tea was distributed and the maid left, Colleen was ready to broach the subject again.

"Your visit?"

"Yes. I have been worried since you took the tumble down the stairs. I had not heard much, just that you were recovering. No one has visited other than Bridgerton."

She sipped her tea, trying to figure out just why he was commenting on that and why he would care.

"Yes, although I told Lady Victoria not to worry about that. She insisted on keeping the house quiet for me."

"I heard it was your husband who forbade anyone to enter."

She cocked her head and studied the young duke, wondering at his motives. "I doubt that Sebastian would do that. But if he did, he must have good reason." And she would get to the bottom of it the moment she saw him again. "You must be mistaken, Your Grace."

With aggravated movements, he rose and began to pace. "I do not know about anyone else, but I have been here on three separate occasions to check on you and was turned away all three times."

Alarmed at his actions and the tone in his voice, Colleen tried to calm him. "No one was permitted in."

"And Bridgerton threatened me. Me!" He stopped, placed a hand on each hip and stared down at her. His blue grey eyes narrowed as he studied her. A chill shivered down her spine. "That wasn't what I wanted to talk about. I just...I want you to know that if you ever find yourself in trouble, you can call on me for assistance."

She didn't know what to say. All the ins and outs of society were still a mystery to Colleen, but she was sure the duke didn't run around pledging to protect all women. She nodded.

He sighed. "I know it seems strange. But just remember you can count on me for any help you should need."

Without another word, he quit the room, leaving Colleen with an uneasy feeling that if Sebastian wasn't right about the duke, there was something else very wrong.

CRCBCR

Sally had just finished with Colleen's hair when her husband walked into her bedroom. Watching him in the mirror, she noted the tension around his mouth.

"That will be all, Sally. I will call when I am ready to dress."

As soon as the maid was out of the room, Colleen turned to Sebastian. He apparently had just returned. He had not had his bath or shaved for the evening. Anger rolled off him in waves.

"What is wrong?"

"Did you have a visitor while I was out today, dear?" Sarcasm dripped from his voice, making the endearment anything but sweet.

Confused, she studied him. He was fairly quivering with the need to shout, and the fact that he didn't amazed her. "Yes. Ethingham stopped by to check on me."

A little of the tension seemed to dissolve from his face as he stepped forward. "I gave word that he was not to be admitted. I would like it if you would respect my wishes."

She measured his words, trying to decipher just what was going on in his head. "Why?"

"Why did I bar him from the house, or why would I not like you to see him?"

She cocked her head. "Both."

"I don't trust him."

She waited, thinking he would elaborate, but when he didn't she asked, "Do you not trust me?"

His eyes widened, surprise stealing over his features. "Of course I do."

"Then why would you worry?"

"Word has it you were alone. That you and His Grace were alone in the parlor for about thirty minutes."

"It was actually a much shorter amount of time with the door left open." She stood, her own anger building. "What I would like to know is why you feel the need to have spies watch your wife?"

He crossed his arms over his chest and glared at her. "I do not have spies watching you."

"Then how do you know about Ethingham?"

He ignored her and frowned harder. "In thirty minutes, anything could have happened."

His outburst sent a shard of ice slicing at her heart. "Anything?"

For a second, panic shone in his eyes, but it vanished just as fast as it appeared. "Yes. Anything. You are naïve in the ways of the ton, Colleen, but in thirty minutes, even in the front parlor, a lot can happen."

She swallowed. "I know. I understand what you are trying to explain to me, as if I were a simpleton. But what I want to know is why you don't trust me."

He scoffed. "I trust you. I don't trust him or his influence."

"No, you do not trust me. If you did, you wouldn't worry about Ethingham or his influence on me."

"Don't be ridiculous. I trust you. I was just...looking out for my interests."

She should have been comforted by the note of desperation in his voice. Something was there, something he was hiding. Then it crashed down on her, sending a wave of regret and pain rolling through her.

"It is Elizabeth. You don't trust me because of your first wife." And if he couldn't trust her, after all these weeks of her proving herself to him, what was left? She thought she had gained a measure of trust, something to hold on to until Sebastian finally realized he loved her. It was not going to happen. Although she had changed much in the last few months, the love for her husband growing every day as did the child they had created, there was one thing she would not do. She would not beg for love.

"No, Colleen, it is not Elizabeth. I am trying to protect what is mine."

What was his? His possession, his wife, but not his love. She did not care how many times he used the endearment, he had not meant it. She turned away from him, trying not to let him see the hurt he had caused. She did have pride, no matter how tattered it might be. A lump rose in her throat. She wanted to believe him, she did. But she knew in the end it would not happen. She would end up more hurt than now, even though that was hard to imagine.

"Colleen, it has nothing to do with her, and I trust you. I do."

He stepped closer. She could feel the heat of him against her back. The need to lean into him, share that warmth, revel in his touch almost overwhelmed her good thinking. But she straightened her spine and bolstered her will. "It has everything to do with it. If you trusted me, you would never have asked."

"I will always ask because I fear no man can resist you."

The compliment held no appeal. It was just more empty drivel he had learned in order to seduce.

She turned to face him, allowing him to see the anger she felt, and he took a step back. "I will not spend the rest of my life proving myself to you, Sebastian." She advanced on him as he continued to back away, his expression turning darker with each step. "I will not pay for your first wife's mistakes, and I will not spend the rest of my life loving a man who cannot return the sentiment." She hated that her voice quivered on the last word. Swallowing, she looked away. "Until you can accept that I am good enough for you, I will not be accompanying you out. I will not have you hovering over me, waiting for me to make a mistake."

She stepped back from him. He reached for her, but she moved away from his touch. "Colleen. I don't think you are not good enough."

"Until you accept me, you will always leave me with doubts."

She felt his hesitation, thought maybe, just maybe there was hope, but it deflated a moment later as she heard him walk to his door.

"I will tell Mother to go on without me."

She looked back over her shoulder and fought another wave of sympathy, the need to comfort. He looked so pained, so rejected that she wanted to take back every word.

"No, you go ahead. There is no reason for you to stay here."

He opened his mouth, but she stopped him. "Really, there is no reason for you to be here, and at the moment I do not want to see you."

He studied her, his eyes pleading with her for something she could not understand. If he would take it back, declare his love, tell her he never wanted her to leave, that he wanted to spend the rest of his days with her, she would gladly forget all his words. But the declaration never came. And truthfully, she wasn't sure she would believe him if he said it now. With a curt nod, he left her. When she heard the click of the door, she sank down on the floor, covered her mouth with her hand and began to cry.

CR CB CR

Sebastian shifted his weight from foot to foot, his mind telling him that everything would be okay, while his heart kept sending out warnings. Warnings that he was losing Colleen.

He nodded to an acquaintance but barely noticed who it was.

"You need to smile, Sebastian, or else everyone will think there is something wrong." His mother's admonition rankled.

He glanced at her and then back at the dancers. "Why would anyone think anything is wrong?"

"You appear without Colleen, tell us she is not feeling well, but you are not staying home. Not your normal pattern. Then you look at every passerby in this ball as if they had done something personal to you." She sighed. "Sebastian, this has the earmarks of wounded male all over it. Why don't you leave and talk things out with your wife?"

He longed to do that. However, Colleen had been the one who said they had nothing to discuss, and he had let her be. It was driving him mad. He wanted to beat his chest and roar. Why had he not told Colleen the whole story, everything, so she could protect herself? It was the most asinine thing he had ever done, standing there while she yelled at him. But he could not help it. She had admitted her love, not with a declaration, but with one comment.

I will not spend the rest of my life loving a man who cannot return the sentiment.

Every thought, every argument flew out of his mind at the moment Colleen had uttered that statement. He wasn't even sure if she realized she said it. A strange mixture of joy and fear had swept through him, grabbing him by the heart. It had yet to let go. He should have gone back, told her of his feelings, but she was not ready. She did not believe a word he said, and if he said he loved her now, she would think he was just trying to win her back. He was going to have to prove it to her.

"There is something wrong. I am at this blasted ball and my wife is at home."

"And whose fault is that?" Victoria cocked her head and smiled at him. "Quit being so stubborn and go back home and apologize."

"How do you know it is my fault?"

"You are a man, darling. It is always your fault."

Surprised, he laughed. He was about to agree until he spotted Daniel signaling that he had found the duke.

"I will return home soon, but first I need to have a little discussion with someone. Daniel will see you and Anna home."

She didn't argue, although he knew she wanted to. Thanking heaven for her discretion, he bid her goodbye and met up with Daniel in the hallway.

"He's in the library, although he is a bit on the nervous side," Daniel said.

"He should be. I am going to beat him to a bloody pulp."

Daniel grabbed hold of him by his upper arm. "Don't do it. Don't create a scandal. Colleen does not need that right now. You do not need that right now."

He was right. Sebastian worked hard to calm his anger to a low boil and led Daniel down the hallway. When he came to the door, he hesitated, drew in a deep breath and opened the door.

At first, he didn't see Ethingham. A movement by the window caught his eye, and he zeroed in on him. Surprisingly, the man was not dressed for the ball. He looked as if he'd not changed out of his riding clothes. He stared out the rain-soaked window appearing as if he'd lost his best friend.

"Your Grace."

He turned to face Sebastian and Daniel. The usual jovial demeanor was not there. Anger darkened his eyes, his jaw clenched as if in an effort not to yell, his lips pulled back in a sneer. The man facing them was not Ethingham, the seducer of many widows and chorus girls, and definitely not easily swept under the rug. This was the duke.

"What the bloody hell are you doing here, Penwyth?"

The anger he had pushed back roared to the surface. "What business is it of yours, Ethingham?"

"Your woman is at home. Alone."

"If you think to entice her into a liaison, you have made a grave error."

Of all the reactions Sebastian expected, it was not the burst of laughter from Ethingham. "Oh, that is rich. You think I am trying to lure your lady away."

"Ethingham." He growled the man's name and almost jumped over the chaise lounge to get to him. Very easily he could picture his hands wrapping around the bastard's neck.

"Sebastian." Again, Daniel stopped him, grabbing his arm and stepping in front of him. "If you two are finished, I think you owe Sebastian an explanation."

The duke choked on another laugh but seemed able to finally restrain his reaction. "Thanks, Penwyth. I needed that. I don't think I have laughed like that in a long time."

"Ethingham," Daniel said, his own voice a warning that he was pushing his luck. He'd released Sebastian and moved close to the duke. Curling his fingers into his palms, Sebastian waited for Ethingham to bait him again.

"Right. First, I would never try to seduce a woman who is so obviously in love with her husband and vice versa." He paused, apparently waiting for Sebastian's agreement. When he nodded, the duke smiled. "And Penwyth, although it is practiced by many of the ton, I don't dally with first cousins. I protect them."

CROSCR

Colleen sighed, sipping her chocolate, and looked out her window. The rain had moved across London, dampening the streets, feeding into the sadness that gripped her soul. Maybe she was being irrational or demanding, but she wanted Sebastian's trust. She wanted his love.

Sighing again, she moved away from the window, thinking that maybe she had been a bit rash. Sebastian was being protective and acting a bit jealous. She needed to remember he was stuck in the marriage as much as she was. Everything was so new, so scary. There was a chance he was confused. Or maybe, just maybe, he was in love.

She stopped in the middle of her room. All the sounds, the street clatter, the crackling fire, faded into the background as she assessed Sebastian's behavior of the last few weeks.

As the memories tumbled over each other, hope sparked in her heart. He was acting irrationally because he was in love with her. His jealousy was his own worry that *she* didn't love him. Excitement filled her as she thought again, trying to comprehend his mind. She knew then she needed to talk to him, discuss it. Waiting would drive her mad. She looked down at her wrapper. There was no way she could go to the ball now. The rain had stopped, but by the time she dressed, Sebastian could be on his way home. She worried her lower lip with her teeth as she thought about her choices. Then it struck her.

She could send him a note, urging him home, telling him she must speak to him now. Sebastian was predictable enough that he would hurry home because of a summons from her.

Before she could reach the bellpull, the door opened. Aunt Prudence stood in the doorway with a gun in her hand pointed at Colleen's heart.

Chapter Eighteen

Colleen's breath tangled in her throat as her heart beat against her chest so hard she was amazed it didn't break right through. Prudence shut the door and locked it.

"Prudence?" She had to think, but it was hard because every ounce of blood had drained out of her head from fear. "Is there something I can do for you?"

"Surprised?" she asked sarcastically. "I wager you are. No one ever expects the woman of being the one. They all think we are stupid."

"The one what, Prudence?" Cold fingers trailed down Colleen's spine, and she fought off the shiver it caused.

She laughed. The hysterical sound bounced off the walls. Madness shone in her grey eyes. "You don't even know. Sebastian didn't tell you, did he? Men never do." Her expression moved from gleeful to thunderous. "They think we can't handle anything other than picking out gowns and being vessels for their lust."

Colleen fought the urge to laugh nervously. It was all she could do not to fall into sobs in front of this madwoman.

"Do you know how I found out we had no money?" Prudence stared at her, waiting. Colleen shook her head. "I was refused credit at the modiste's. It was embarrassing. Thank goodness no one was there to see it, but imagine being turned away like that."

Colleen swallowed past the queasiness caused by her unsettled stomach. In that instant, she remembered the babe nestled in her. Safe, for now. She wanted to shield him from this, put her hands over her abdomen and protect him, but she didn't want to draw attention to the fact she was pregnant. Who knew what this woman was capable of?

"So James spent all your money. Did you speak with Sebastian about this?"

"No. Grovel to him for money, I think not!" Her eyes narrowed, and the madness turned to anger. "And you would like that, Lady Penwyth, wouldn't you?"

Colleen shook her head again.

"Oh, yes you would. You think you can do no wrong. Sebastian thinks the same thing. I have seen the way he looks at you. He thinks himself in love with you. That won't last. It never does. Soon he will leave your bed for a bought whore. Men can never stay faithful."

Colleen kept silent, not knowing if something she said would set Prudence off.

"But I will be the Countess of Penwyth soon enough. As soon as I kill you and frame your husband."

CRCBCR

"First cousin?" Sebastian's mind blanked of all thought. He never expected...

Ethingham smirked. "Yes. Colleen is the daughter of Jane Macgregor, who was Lady Jane, my aunt."

Daniel stepped up to stand beside him. "Are you telling me that Colleen is a granddaughter of a duke?"

Ethingham nodded. "And the cousin of a duke."

"Oh, Lord." Sebastian sat with a thump on a chair.

"My aunt ran off with William Macgregor, married for love. She had the added benefit of escaping my grandfather. My grandfather, being true to form, cut her off without a penny to her name. Apparently, Aunt Jane could have cared less. When my father came into the dukedom, I knew he never tried to locate his sister. He saw her running away with a man he considered beneath her station good reason to ignore her."

Sebastian shook his head, trying to get his brain back into working order. "How? How did you know?"

"It's the eyes. There is a portrait of her mother hanging in the ballroom of my estate. I had to dig it out when I took over the dukedom. She has her mother's eyes."

"And why were you spending time with James?" Daniel asked.

"Ah, well, I needed to pump someone for information, and other people would have been suspicious. James talks up a storm if you give him enough brandy."

Before Sebastian could respond the door burst open and Jenkins hurried to his side. A harried footman followed him, trying to catch his arm to drag him out.

"It is okay. He is with us," Daniel said, and ushered the footman out. "What is it, Jenkins?"

He studied Sebastian's face then shot a look at Ethingham. "I guess you know about Lady Penwyth and him being related?"

Sebastian nodded.

Jenkins sighed. "Well, I have another bit of news that may interest you. Watch found a floater a couple nights ago. Jasper. Vile man." He made a face. "Known for odd jobs."

"Odd jobs? As in killing people?"

Jenkins' dark brown eyes narrowed as if he could see the dead man before him. "Nasty bit of goods. But one of the things they found in his possession was a piece of paper which had the name and address of a person who struck me as odd. When they looked over his flat, they found more money than Jasper should have had on him. The man was a gambler and drunkard."

"So what does this have to do with the investigation?" Daniel asked.

"Jasper was the killer," Sebastian said, a chill passing over his heart. "And the person paying him?"

"Prudence Ware."

CR CB CR

Colleen sat in the chair, wondering when Prudence was planning on killing her, if she ever was. She'd spent the last ten minutes ranting about the lack of funds in her life. Surely, someone would come soon. It wasn't like the staff to not check in on her, especially since this was her first night alone since her fall. She glanced at the door.

"Do not think anyone will come to your rescue. I drugged your guards."

"My guards?"

"Yes. Such a nuisance but a smart man. Your husband posted a couple of footman outside your door tonight. I made sure they had some hot chocolate, filled with laudanum of course."

Woodenly, Colleen nodded. As dread settled over her, she studied the older woman. The cool, calculated look in her eyes told Colleen all she needed to know. Prudence was mad, but she wasn't stupid.

"So where was I? Ah, yes. I had a plan. My daughter, the mouse, never took. She could not make a good marriage. Even with an excellent dowry, I think she would have had to compromise herself to get a man to marry her. And maybe not even then." A self-satisfied smirk curled Prudence's lips and then she laughed—a tinkle really. Colleen did not repress the shiver this time. "So, back to my plan. I prepared to kill them over a period of time but then Gilbert married, and I could not waste time. I had to kill one right after the other. I knew it would look suspicious but that couldn't be helped. Sebastian was really the easiest. We all knew, as most of London did, that the man had lost his handle on the world because of that slut of a wife. So just a tap on the head and he would freeze to death.

"But that didn't work, did it? You found him, nursed him back to health and then he married you. And here you are, two months later, breeding with his child."

Panic swelled as her stomach muscles clenched. Oh, no! She knew about the baby.

Prudence smiled at her, the sight so evil Colleen had to close her eyes.

"Yes, I know about the baby. Not too hard. All I had to do was bribe a few upstairs maids with a silly story of wanting to surprise you with a baby gift. They told me everything I needed to know."

"You did this for money? Prudence, Sebastian will do anything you want, give you anything."

Prudence frowned. It wasn't much better than the smile.

"He probably would. But that will not help me. I need a title. Cicely will never make a match as just a cousin of an earl. She needs to be the daughter of an earl."

What she needed was another mother, but Colleen kept that to herself. "Sebastian would provide a dowry."

Prudence snorted. "You don't understand, Lady Penwyth. No man is going to marry her without a father with a title. There is nothing she can offer a man."

"It is always sad to hear what people think of me, especially my mother."

Both of them whipped their heads in the direction of the door that connected to Sebastian's chamber. Cicely stood at the threshold, dressed in black, her brown hair pulled tight behind her head, her face looking as if her world had ended. She had heard everything, Colleen thought. Poor girl.

"Cicely." Prudence sounded surprised but not alarmed that her daughter had joined them. "You understand, don't you?"

Cicely moved into the room, casting a glance at Colleen as if trying to check to see if she was okay. Colleen nodded, and Cicely turned her attention back to her mother. "Yes, unfortunately, I do understand. I understand I am not the daughter you expected, a woman who is a diamond of the first water." She took a few steps closer to her mother. "I also know about your embarrassing attempt to buy me a husband a few years ago. You and everyone else think I am stupid, think I know nothing." She drew in a deep breath and the pain in her eyes cut right to Colleen's soul. "But I am smart. When you started meeting with that man, I knew there was something up. I followed you here tonight because I cannot let you do this."

Prudence wavered, her hand shaking on the gun. Cicely was close enough to grab her. Colleen held her breath waiting, hoping that Cicely had a plan.

"I did it for *you*," Prudence screamed.

Cicely swallowed, the only show of nerves Colleen had witnessed from the woman. "I did not want it."

"You should marry and marry well."

Cicely cocked her head to the side. "Like you did, Mother? Did it bring you happiness?"

With a growl, her mother raised the gun and pointed it at Cicely's chest.

CRCBCR

Sebastian was in the foyer, racing toward the stairs when he heard first one gunshot and then another. His blood ran cold, his heart dropping to his feet. She couldn't be dead. He wouldn't allow it.

As he reached the top of the stairs, he ran down the hall, servants, the duke and Daniel hard on his heels. Without a thought to his own safety, he pushed open the doors and burst into the room. The smell of gunpowder filled his senses as did the metallic scent of blood. His stomach roiled.

He glanced wildly around, looking for Colleen. He found her on her knees next to a prone body.

"Colleen!"

She looked up, relief lighting up her face. He thought it was the sweetest thing he had ever seen. "Sebastian."

When he reached her, he pulled her into his arms. "Are you all right, love? Did anything happen to you?" He ran his hands over her body, checking for wounds, wondering where the blood was coming from.

"Sebastian." She pulled out of his arms. "It's Cicely. Prudence shot her."

It was then that he noticed the young woman was the body on the floor. "Prudence?"

"Dead. But I think that we can save Cicely."

Just then a moan emitted from Cicely. Both of them looked down at the woman as her eyes fluttered open.

"Colleen," Cicely said. Her voice was so weak, Colleen had to lean closer to hear. "You are all right? She did not hurt you?"

Colleen's eyes filled with tears and she took Cicely's hand in hers. Brushing hair off Cicely's face as a mother would a child, she smiled. "No, I am fine .You saved me."

"Mother?" Cicely asked.

Colleen glanced at Sebastian who looked at Daniel. He shook his head, telling Sebastian Prudence was dead.

"She didn't make it."

Cicely licked her lips and tried to swallow. "I just wish I would have figured it out sooner."

Then she went limp and Colleen called out her name.

Sebastian checked Cicely's pulse, which was beating strong, indicating the woman had just fainted.

He gathered Colleen into his arms. "She is okay, she just fainted. We'll get the doctor here as fast as we can."

She nodded against his chest. He stood, then pulled her up off the floor.

"I want to stay here."

"Let Daniel take care of that. He can handle wounds."

"But—"

"You will just be in the way."

That convinced her to leave. He picked her up and carried her to his room. As the staff, instructed by Daniel and Ethingham, cleaned up the room, he sat in a chair beside the fire, his wife settled in his lap. His nerves calming, his heartbeat finally returning to normal. He knew he could handle anything now that Colleen was safe.

Epilogue

Two weeks later, Colleen sat up first thing in the morning, promptly leaned over the bed and vomited. Sebastian was there next to her, holding her hair out of the way and praying that for once the woman would quit being so stubborn. For the last weeks, most mornings had been spent with his wife ill. He had tried to get her to see Watkins, but she had refused.

When she had finished the last of the dry heaves, he pulled her back in bed, insisting she settle against the pillows. He did not like it at all. The woman was sick in the mornings, refused to eat certain foods, all the while asking for the strangest things, and broke down in tears at the slightest comment. He had thought at first it had been the memories of what had happened that night in her room with Prudence, but she kept assuring him it was not.

The tale Cicely and Colleen told him, of how her mother was going to kill Colleen and frame him for the murder, of how Cicely had come prepared and only ended up with a shoulder wound because Prudence was not quick enough on the draw, had chilled him to the bone. Both she and Cicely seemed to come to terms with it, talking for long hours. Sebastian had agreed to bequest a dowry upon her, but Cicely said with a murderess for a mother and a gambler for a father, there wasn't much hope.

Ethingham had been around a lot, too. Once they told Colleen the story, she smiled at the duke with tears in her eyes and said one word. "Cousin."

His Grace apparently thought it very important to spend all his time with his newfound family member, and Sebastian understood it to a degree. But it was kind of irritating to have to share her with another male. And the fact his mother had acted unsurprised and gave His Grace free run of their house was even more aggravating. She'd figured the whole thing out weeks earlier.

He studied Colleen. He still couldn't believe she was safe, that she was his. He never again wanted to go through that fear of losing her. But something was bothering her. She was pale, losing weight, and he would not stand for it.

He climbed out of bed and pulled on his dressing gown. "I am going to send for Dr. Watkins."

"Sebastian. I have told you, there is nothing wrong with me." She spoke in a tone that told him she thought he was acting like a child.

"Ha. You will see him, and that is the end of that."

He turned on his heel and stalked to the bellpull.

"Sebastian."

The resoluteness in her voice stopped him. He turned and faced her. A small smile played about her lips, and he wanted to kiss away anything that was bothering her. He wanted her to feel safe again, dammit.

"Come here." She reached for her spectacles as he approached the bed. She patted the bed and he sat. Taking his hand, she placed it on her stomach. Her eyes sparkled with wonder. "There is nothing wrong with me that seven or so more months can't solve."

For a second, he couldn't figure out what she was talking about. And then it hit him. He glanced down at his hand gently rubbing her belly. Joy filled him as he thought of his child growing inside her.

"You're breeding?"

He looked up at her. Tears had gathered in her eyes.

"Yes."

He couldn't stop the smile that curved his lips. He drew her into his arms and kissed her. Pulling back, he captured her gaze. Tears rolled down her cheeks and he wiped them away with his thumb.

"I love you, Colleen."

She smiled. "I know. I love you too, Sebastian."

He settled beside her and hauled her back into his arms. "Seven months is not a long time. We have a lot to plan."

"Sebastian there is plenty of time to plan."

"Ohhh, no you don't, Colleen. We may have fallen into this accidentally, but from here on out, I want no more surprises."

Her laughter filled the air around him as joy warmed his heart. Sebastian had found his countess, his love, even if by accident.

About the Author

Born to an Air Force family at an Army hospital, Melissa has always been a little bit screwy. She was further warped by her years of watching *Monty Python* and her strange family. Her love of romance novels developed after accidentally picking up a Linda Howard book. After becoming hooked, she read close to three hundred novels in one year, deciding that romance was her true calling instead of the literary short stories and suspenses she had been writing. After many attempts, she realized that romantic comedy, or at least romance with a comedic edge, was where she was destined to be. Influences in her writing come from Nora Roberts, Jenny Cruise, Susan Andersen, Amanda Quick, Jayne Anne Krentz, Julia Quinn, Christina Dodd and Lori Foster. Since her first release in 2004, Melissa has had close to twenty short stories, novellas and novels released with six different publishers in a variety of genres and time periods.

Since she was a military brat, she vowed never to marry military. Alas, Fate always has her way with mortals. Melissa's husband is an Air Force major, and together they have their own military brats, two girls, and they live wherever the military sticks them. Which, she is sure, will always involve heat and bugs only seen on the Animal Discovery Channel. In her spare time, she reads, complains about bugs, travels, cooks, reads some more, watches her DVD collections of *Arrested*

Development and *Seinfeld,* and tries to convince her family that she truly is a *delicate genius.* She has yet to achieve her last goal.

She has always believed that romance and humor go hand in hand. Love can conquer all and as Mark Twain said, "Against the assault of laughter, nothing can stand." Combining the two, she hopes she gives her readers a thrilling love story, filled with chuckles along the way, and a happily ever after finish.

To learn more about Melissa, please visit www.melissaschroeder.net. Send an email to Melissa at Melissa@melissaschroeder.net or join her Yahoo! group to join in the fun with other readers as well as Melissa. For chat, http://groups.yahoo.com/group/melissaschroederchat, and for news

http://groups.yahoo.com/group/melissaschroedernews/.

Look for these titles

Now Available

Grace Under Pressure
A Little Harmless Sex
The Accidental Countess
Lessons in Seduction
The Seduction of Widow McEwan

Coming Soon:

Devil's Rise
A Little Harmless Pleasure
A Little Harmless Obsession
The Spy Who Loved Her
A Little Harmless Addiction
The Last Detail

What is a lady to do when her chosen rake changes her lessons in seduction to lessons of love?

Lessons in Seduction
© *2007 Melissa Schroeder*

Cicely Ware understands how society works. At the age of twenty-six, she has been around long enough to know that she is doomed to spinsterhood. But she refuses to go without ever knowing what it is like to be with a man. So she comes up with a wonderful plan to find a rake to teach her, complete with a list of possibilities. At the top of that list sits Douglas the Duke of Ethingham.

When he asks Lady Cicely to waltz, Douglas never expected her to request seduction, or that it would intrigue him quite as much. With each glance, each smile, each touch, he finds himself falling under her spell, unable to resist her lure. In her he finds a soul mate, someone as lonely as he is, who understands his pain, and will give herself to him without demands or expectations.

But as he finds himself falling in love, he also discovers a wicked plot to kill Lady Cicely. As they race to discover who wants her dead, they fall deeper in love, leaving them to decide if the lessons in seduction could lead to a lifetime of happiness.

Available now in ebook from Samhain Publishing.

Enjoy the following excerpt from Lessons in Seduction...

Cicely's heart stuttered at the deep sound of Douglas' voice. Oh, no. No. No. *No.*

She closed her eyes against the sudden press of tears and fought the urge to stomp her foot—which would have been difficult since she was sitting. Besides, the barefoot stomp was never as satisfactory as a heeled one. The heeled one made a very satisfying thump. She allowed a frown to disfigure her face. It was dark, what did she care? Douglas thought she was that Lady Tremount. Or some other trollop. She would almost think the situation humorous, if she didn't find it so horribly painful. She'd done nothing so hideous in her life as to deserve this.

Cicely didn't open her eyes when she felt him sink next to her on the sofa. The cushion flexed under his weight. She waited for Douglas to realize he'd mistaken her for another woman as he slipped his hand over her cold, clenched fist.

"Awfully quiet, my lady. I've never known you to be so reserved."

She opened her eyes. She was positive any moment he would guess her identity and his horror would be too much to bear. But she would, just as she had a few nights before, face it. It was best to confront his disgust for her and use it as a weapon to remind herself what he thought of her. She turned her head, drawing back when she realized he'd moved closer. She blinked, then blinked again.

With the drapes closed, the room was near pitch black, and it was understandable he didn't know who she was. He expected someone else.

Douglas trailed his incredibly warm hand up her arm, his fingers gliding over the side of her bound breasts then farther up to cup her face. Gently, he pulled her closer. His heat surrounded her, warmed her, mesmerized her.

When she was just inches away from pressing her lips to his, he paused to say, "I've never known you to play reticent before. I have to say, I quite like it."

His breath warmed her face as he spoke. Guilt held her tongue. She should tell him and end this embarrassing façade. A moment later, he brushed his lips against hers and every thought of righting his misconception dissolved. A liquid-silver thrill shot through her, sending her heart beating out of control, her head spinning. Sighing, she leaned into him. This was a fear she could learn to love.

Apparently thinking it an invitation—because truly it had been—Douglas raised his other hand to frame her face completely and deepened the kiss. She twined her arms behind his neck and returned the kiss with all the passion in her heart. The feel of his tongue against her closed mouth caused her to gasp. Before she knew what he was about, his tongue was inside, tasting her...tempting her.

God help her, she was putty in his large, capable hands.

She moaned. He slipped his hands down her body to her waist then lifted her, placing her on his lap. Warmth seeped into every pore, her flesh heating, her body vibrating. This wasn't proper, that she knew. Still...

She felt his heart beat through his shirt and jacket. That he thought her someone else didn't matter. All that mattered was that at this one moment, the man she desired—and God help her, loved—desired her in return. Her, a nobody who barely turned the head of even the most boring of men. But this man, a gorgeous, seductive charmer, was kissing her as if his life depended on it. Somewhere in the back of her mind a bit of her better judgment prodded. With determination, she pushed the doubts away. She just wanted to be touched...to feel, to be felt.

He slid his hands to her back, urging her to him. She shifted her weight, rubbing her chest against his. Even through the fabric of her gown and the layers of her binding, the friction hardened her nipples. Her bones melted as he moved from her mouth to the delicate skin just below her jaw. His lips felt so good. They burned a trail wherever they touched and when they slid from one spot to another, the fire lingered, pushing deep past her defenses, ingraining in her memory. Wanting— needing—more, she tipped her head to one side allowing him better access to her throat. He murmured something against her skin that she couldn't grasp, but it thrilled her just the same. He moved on to her ear as she began to shift against him. The scrape of his teeth against her lobe had her moaning his name and threading her fingers through his hair.

GREAT cheap fun

Discover eBooks!

THE FASTEST WAY TO GET THE HOTTEST NAMES

Get your favorite authors on your favorite reader, long before they're
out in print! Ebooks from Samhain go wherever you go, and work with
whatever you carry—Palm, PDF, Mobi, and more.

SAMHAIN
puBLISHING ltd

WWW.SAMHAINPUBLISHING.COM